GARLIC & the VAMPIRE

Garlic & the Vampire

Bree Paulsen

Quill Tree Books
Imprints of HarperCollinsPublishers

QUILL TREE BOOKS IS AN IMPRINT OF HARPERCOLLINS PUBLISHERS.

HARPERALLEY IS AN IMPRINT OF HARPERCOLLINS PUBLISHERS.

GARLIC AND THE VAMPIRE

WWW.HARPERALLEY.COM

ISBN 978-0-06-299509-4 (TRADE BDG.)

ISBN 978-0-06-299508-7 (PBK.)

THE ARTIST USED ADOBE PHOTOSHOP AND PROCREATE TO CREATE THE DIGITAL ILLUSTRATIONS FOR THIS BOOK.

TYPOGRAPHY BY DAVID CURTIS

22 23 24 25 EP 10 9 8 7 6 5 4 3

FIRST EDITION

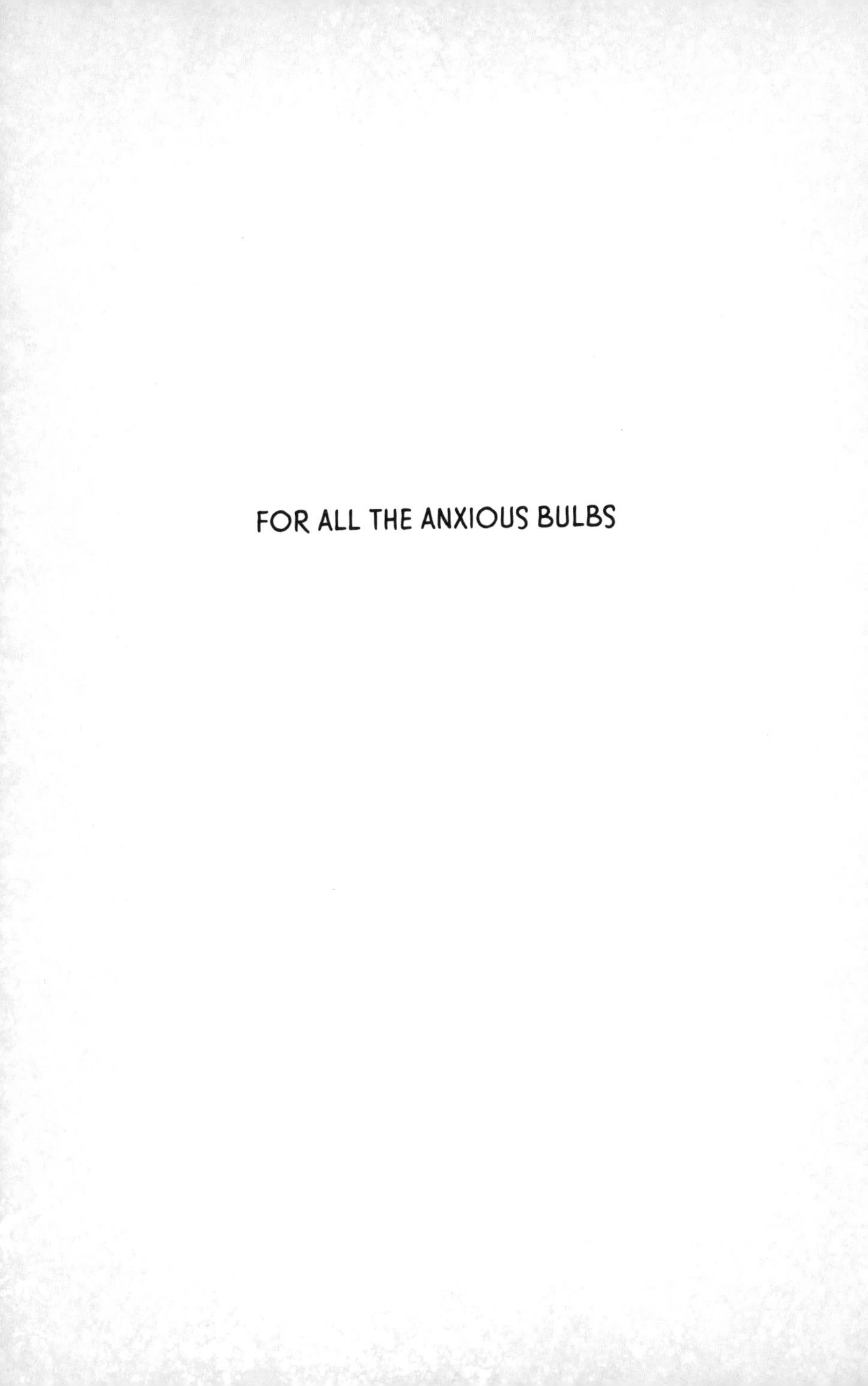

FOR ALL THE ANXIOUS BULBS

chapter one

MMM...
yawn

I tried to wake you
so it's your fault if
you're late today.
-Carrot

WHA—

NO!
NO!
NO!

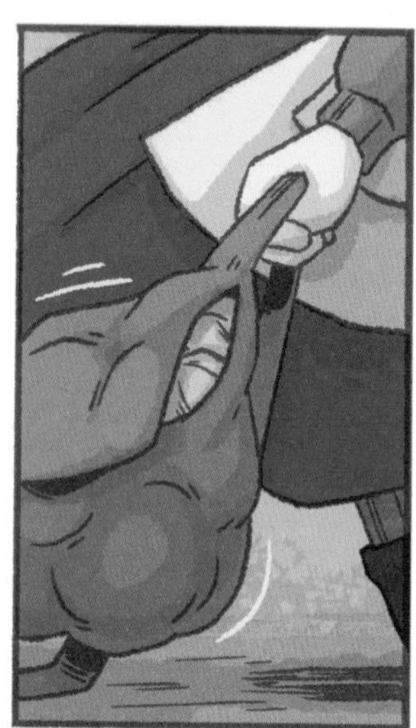

tuft
tuft

tuft
tuft

gasp

ACK!
I CAN'T BE LATE AGAIN!
I'M NEVER GONNA HEAR THE END OF IT FROM CARROT!

tuft
tuft

HA
HA
HA

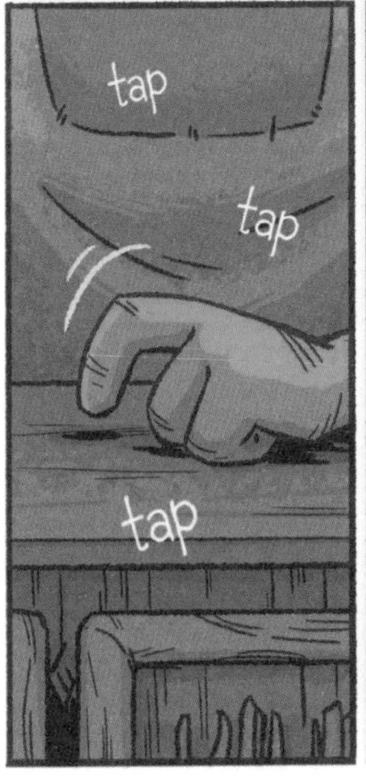
tap
tap
tap

tap

CRIKEY!
SORRY!

WHOA!
OH MY!

SORRY!
SORRY!
SORRY!
UH, GOOD MORNING.

WAH!
SORRY!

WHOA!
WATCH IT!

thump
thump

slide

sigh

KNOCKED ON YOUR DOOR. **NO ANSWER.**

SHOUTED YOUR NAME. **NOTHING.**

TRIED SHAKING YOU AWAKE AND YOU **FINALLY** MUTTERED SOMETHING.

I'M SO SORRY, WITCH AGNES—

MA'AM!

I WON'T BE LATE AGAIN!

HEH, HMM...
YEAH... I DON'T THINK SHE NOTICED.

ACK! SHE'S SO MAD AT ME!
FURIOUS!
nod nod
YEP, SO FURIOUS.

SHE'S FUMING.
OH NO! I KNEW IT!

I'M KIDDING.
SHE'S JUST GLAD YOU'RE HERE.

MAYBE...
I JUST FEEL LIKE SUCH A DISAPPOINTMENT.
I CAN'T REMEMBER THE LAST TIME I WAS NOT LATE.

I'M PRETTY SURE CELERY IS STILL MAD AT ME FOR KNOCKING OVER HIS DISPLAY LAST WEEK.

GLA ARE
HE'LL FORGIVE YOU EVENTUALLY.
pat
pat
I HOPE SO...

I DEFINITELY RECOMMEND THOSE IF YOU'RE MAKING A SAUCE.

THANK YOU! ENJOY!

HERE YOU GO!
LET POTATO AND I KNOW HOW THOSE LATKES TURN OUT, OKAY?

GOODBYE!
SEE YOU NEXT WEEK!

OH, MUST'VE DROPPED ONE.

kick

sft
sft

BONK
AH!

SORRY...

LUCKILY, EVERYTHING IS PACKED UP THIS TIME.

IGNORE HIM.

I CAN'T WAIT TO GET BACK HOME AND TAKE A NAP.

WHAT?
SLEEPING IN WASN'T ENOUGH FOR YA?

TODAY WAS STRESSFUL, **OKAY!**
I NEED ONE.

OKAY, OKAY...

HMM?

chapter two

KRAA!

MORNING!
OH, GOOD MORNING!
AH! YOU'RE STILL ALIVE!
HA HA
OH, SHUSH.
GOOD MORNING.
MORNING!
MORNING!

AH, LOOK AT THAT BIG ONE THERE.
OH, GRAPES! IT'S HUGE!

MMMM...

HELLO,
MY LITTLE
ONES.

HOW
ARE YOU TODAY?
GOOD?

WOULD
YOU LIKE SOME
WATER?
SORRY
IT'S NOT FRESH
RAIN BUT--
HMMM,
TRYING A LITTLE
MAGIC TO HELP
THEM GROW?

NO!
AT LEAST I
DON'T THINK
SO--
I MEAN,
I DON'T KNOW
IF IT'S MAGIC, BUT
I THINK THAT IT
HELPS.

MMM,
LOOKS LIKE IT
IS HELPING.

THANKS...
AND I'M SORRY ABOUT ARRIVING LATE YESTERDAY.
OH, DON'T WORRY ABOUT IT.
IN FACT, IF YOU EVER NEED A BREAK AND WANT TO SKIP IT, JUST LET ME KNOW.
WHAT? BUT—
BUT THIS IS WHAT I'M SUPPOSED TO DO.
I'M SUPPOSED TO HELP YOU WITH THE GARDEN.

THAT MIGHT HAVE BEEN MY INTENT AT FIRST, BUT...

YOU'VE ALL GROWN SO MUCH OVER THE YEARS. YOU'RE NO LONGER MUTE LITTLE HELPERS THAT KEEP ME COMPANY.
YOU ARE YOUR OWN BEINGS WITH THOUGHTS AND FEELINGS.

I'M GLAD YOU STILL ENJOY HELPING ME WITH SO MUCH ATTENTION AND CARE.

SOME OF YOU HAVE EVEN BRANCHED OUT ON YOUR OWN, GROWING HERBS AND OTHER CROPS.

BUT IF YOU EVER WANT TO STOP, TAKE UP SOMETHING NEW, OR GO ON A LITTLE ADVENTURE ON YOUR OWN...
...YOU'RE MORE THAN WELCOME TO DO SO.

HOOOoOOOWL

NOPE, NO ADVENTURES FOR ME.
I LOVE GARDENING.
IT'S NICE AND SAFE.

THEN I'LL LEAVE YOU TO IT.

AND MAYBE SOMEDAY YOU'LL BE ABLE TO DO MAGIC AND BREATHE LIFE INTO YOUR BULBS.

HA, MAYBE...

WAIT, YOU REALLY THINK I'D BE CAPABLE?

I JUST WANT TO HELP THEM GROW.
I DON'T WANT TO BRING THEM TO LIFE!

WHAT IF I ALREADY SOLD GARLIC THAT'S **ALIVE** AND DIDN'T KNOW!
THAT WOULD MEAN—
OH, GRAPES!

OH, SHH— IT'S FINE.
EVEN IF YOU ARE ALREADY CAPABLE, IT ALL DEPENDS ON YOUR INTENT.

YOU WHISPER WITH INTENTIONS OF GROWTH AND GOOD HARVEST, YES?
YOU SHOULD BE FINE.

SHOULD BE?!

WILL! YOU **WILL** BE!

chuckle

WILL YOU STOP STARING LIKE THAT.
YOU'RE WEIRDING ME OUT!
IT'S THERE AGAIN.
HUH? WHAT'S THERE AGAIN?
THE SMOKE.
HMM! THERE IS SMOKE.

I THOUGHT THAT PLACE WAS ABANDONED.

WELL, APPARENTLY NOT ANYMORE.

WHAT ARE Y'ALL POINTING AT?
THERE'S SOMEONE LIVING IN THE CASTLE!
ISN'T IT VACANT?

DOES THAT **LOOK** VACANT TO YOU?!

CELERY, I'M SURE IT'S NOTHING.
MAYBE SOMEONE JUST NEEDED TO TAKE SHELTER FOR A BIT.

OR **NOT!** LOOK AT THE CASTLE!
SOMETHING **TERRIBLE** MUST BE IN THERE!

SO THE WHISPERING AND TALKING ARE FINE AS LONG AS MY INTENTIONS ARE TO HELP THEM GROW.
CORRECT.
GROW LIKE PLANTS...NOT LIKE PEOPLE.
SURE.

OF COURSE THIS IS ASSUMING THAT I CAN ACTUALLY DO THIS KIND OF MAGIC. I DON'T THINK I—

WHAT IS GOING ON OVER THERE?

HMM?

LOOKS LIKE IT HAS SOMETHING TO DO WITH THE SPOOKY CASTLE ON THE HILL.

OH,
GRAPES...

EVERYONE,
CALM DOWN!
CELERY, JUST
BE QUIET FOR A
MOMENT.

WE CAN'T
JUMP TO
CONCLUSIONS.
BUT
WHAT IF—

NOW,
WHAT HAS YOU
ALL VEXED?

THERE'S SOMETHING **TERRIBLE** IN THE CASTLE, AGNES!
LOOKS LIKE SOMEONE IS LIVING THERE, WITCH AGNES.

THERE'S SMOKE RISING FROM THE CHIMNEY, MA'AM.

I SEE...

I'M SURE THERE'S NOTHING WRONG.
BASED ON THE LOOK OF THOSE CLOUDS, SOMEONE IS PROBABLY TAKING REFUGE FROM A POSSIBLE STORM.

SEE, I TOLD YOU.
WE STILL DON'T KNOW FOR SURE.

THOUGH, THERE IS A CHANCE IT IS...

WELL, I DON'T WANT TO ALARM YOU BUT...

...THERE IS A CHANCE IT MIGHT BE A VAMPIRE.

VAMPIRE?!
YOU CAN'T BE SERIOUS.

MY MOTHER TOLD ME ONE RESIDED IN THAT CASTLE A LONG, LONG TIME AGO.

BUT FOR THE PAST CENTURY OR SO, THE CASTLE HAS LAIN VACANT, COLLECTING DUST AND COBWEBS.

IT LOOKED AS THOUGH THE VAMPIRE HAD LEFT...

HE SIMPLY DISAPPEARED.

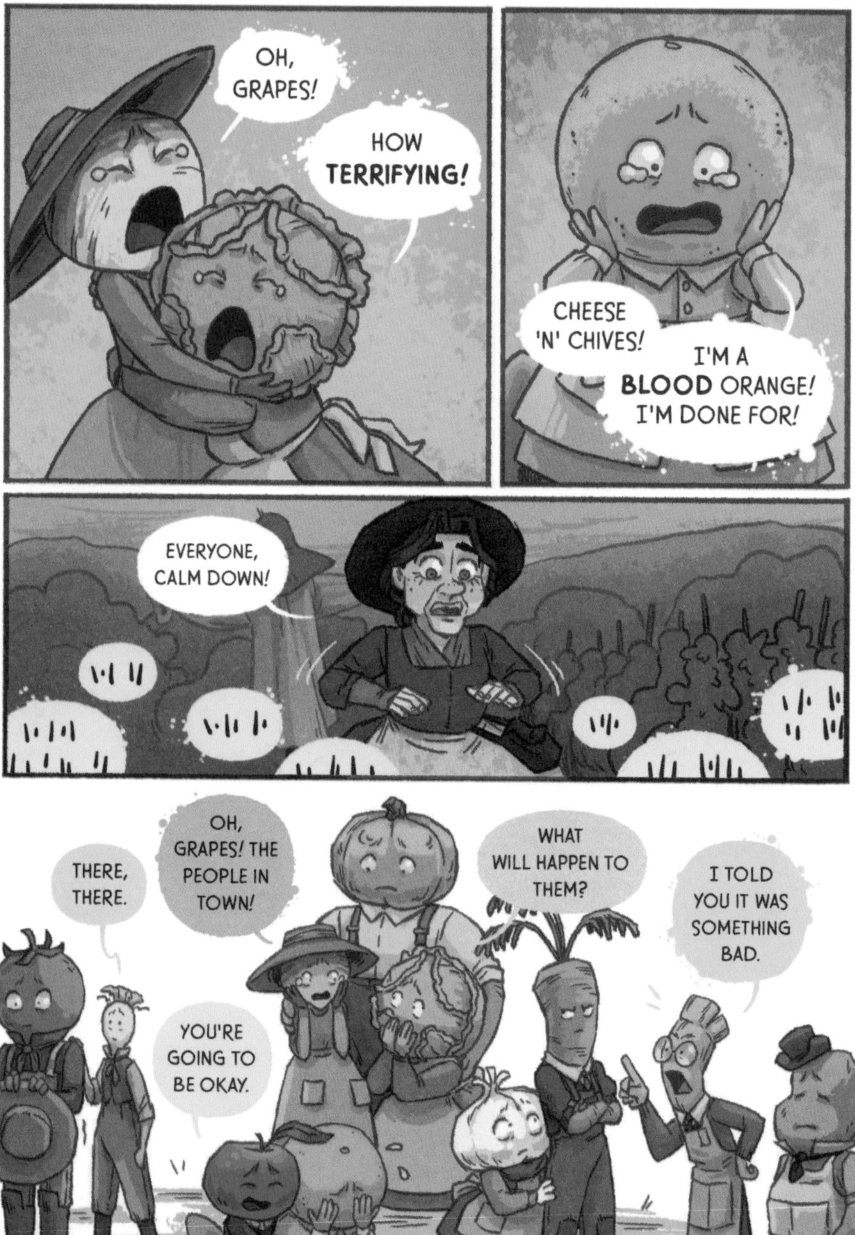

THERE, THERE.

OH, GRAPES! THE PEOPLE IN TOWN!

YOU'RE GOING TO BE OKAY.

WHAT WILL HAPPEN TO THEM?

I TOLD YOU IT WAS SOMETHING BAD.

BUT AGAIN! IT MIGHT NOT BE THE VAMPIRE, JUST A RANDOM TRAVELER.

PUMPKIN AND I CAN SCOPE OUT THE CASTLE AND SEE IF THE VAMPIRE IS THERE.
IT WOULD BE MY HONOR, MA'AM!

THAT IS VERY KIND, BUT THERE'S NO NEED.

BESIDES, IF ANYONE IS GOING UP THERE, SHOULDN'T IT BE GARLIC?
?

NO ONE HAS TO GO UP TO THE CASTLE.

THERE'S A MUCH EASIER SOLUTION.

I HOPE NOT.

chapter three

TAKE A SEAT, EVERYONE.

WITH THIS,
WE'LL BE ABLE TO SEE
IF THERE IS A VAMPIRE IN
THE CASTLE WITHOUT
DETECTION.

ruffle

clk
clk
clk
clk
clk

clk

AAAHH

gasp
OH, GRAPES! OH, GRAPES!

CHEESE 'N' CHIVES! HE LOOKED RIGHT AT US!

DO YOU THINK HE SAW US?!

EVERYONE, STAY CALM.
THERE'S NO NEED TO PANIC, I—

WE HAVE TO DO SOMETHING TO PROTECT THE FOLKS IN TOWN!

SOMEONE SHOULD GO UP THERE AND CONFRONT THIS VAMPIRE.

DOESN'T GARLIC WARD OFF VAMPIRES...?

WHAT? ME?!

GARLIC SHOULD GO AND GET RID OF THE VAMPIRE!

THAT'S TRUE!

YEAH!

CARROT?

GARLIC, I...

EVERYONE STOP! LET US JUST—

BUT PEOPLE HAVE BEEN USING GARLIC AGAINST VAMPIRES FOR CENTURIES.
SHE CAN USE THAT TO HER ADVANTAGE TO DRIVE HIM AWAY OR DESTROY HIM.

DESTROY?!

THAT'S TRUE!
GARLIC, YOU HAVE TO GO.

Shrug
YEAH, GARLIC, YOU **HAVE** TO!
COME ON, GARLIC.

FACE THE VAMPIRE!
ONLY YOU CAN DO THIS.
JUST SAY YOU'LL DO IT!

!

WHAMP
AH!

huff
huff
huff

GARLIC...

CARROT!

OH, GRAPES! WHAT AM I GOING TO DO?

...
pat
pat

GARLIC...
I THINK YOU SHOULD CONFRONT THE VAMPIRE.

IT'S JUST... EVERYONE HAS A POINT.

YOU DO HAVE NATURAL PROTECTION THAT NO ONE ELSE HAS.
I KNOW YOU DON'T WANT TO, BUT YOUR ADVANTAGE MAKES YOU THE BEST PERSON FOR THE JOB.

BUT HOW DO WE KNOW FOR SURE THAT VAMPIRES DON'T LIKE GARLIC?
WHAT IF THAT'S ONLY A RUMOR STARTED BY VAMPIRES?
WHAT IF THEY ACTUALLY LOVE GARLIC!
WHAT IF THEY ACTUALLY FIND IT DELICIOUS!
I HIGHLY DOUBT THAT'S THE CASE, THOUGH YOU ARE QUITE LOVABLE.
CARROT, I'M **SERIOUS**. I'M JUST--
IT'S SO MUCH PRESSURE.
EVERYONE WANTS ME TO DEFEAT THIS VAMPIRE.
ME!

EVEN IF I HAD THE COURAGE, THIS IS ME WE'RE TALKING ABOUT.
I'M GOING TO MESS UP.

THAT MUST BE WHY CELERY SUGGESTED I GO.
HE KNOWS I'LL FAIL.

WHAT? GARLIC, THAT IS ABSURD!
CELERY MAY BE A JERK, BUT I DOUBT HE'D WANT ANYTHING BAD TO HAPPEN TO YOU.

THINK OF THE PEOPLE IN TOWN.

WE VEGGIES MAY BE SAFE, BUT THEY AREN'T.

AND WHO KNOWS WHAT THIS VAMPIRE HAS PLANNED.
HE MIGHT HAVE MINIONS READY TO CARRY OUT HIS EVIL ORDERS...
SIMPLY WAITING FOR HIM TO GIVE THE WORD.

HE MAY WANT TO **DESTROY** THE LAND AND ALL LIFE ON IT BY SHROUDING THE WORLD IN **DARKNESS** SO THAT VAMPIRES CAN **REIGN SUPREME.**

OR NOT!
HE COULD BE COMPLETELY **HARMLESS**, BUT WE WON'T KNOW UNTIL SOMEONE GOES UP TO THE CASTLE.
HA
HA
sigh
I UNDERSTAND IT'S A LOT OF PRESSURE, BUT I REALLY THINK YOU HAVE WHAT IT TAKES TO SUCCEED.
YOU ARE MUCH BRAVER THAN YOU THINK.
YOU CAN DO THIS.

I'LL DO IT.

I'LL
CONFRONT THE
VAMPIRE.

SHE'LL DO IT.
YAY!
OH, GOOD!
YAY!
WOOT!

chapter four

SNIFF
SNIFF

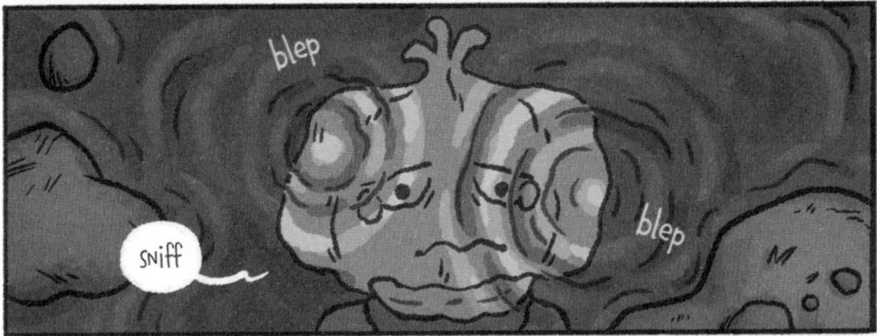

YOU DON'T HAVE TO GO IF YOU DON'T WANT TO.
pat
pat

YOU HEARD WHAT EVERYONE SAID. I'M THE ONLY ONE WHO CAN DO THIS!

THIS VAMPIRE MIGHT HAVE SOME **EVIL PLOT**.
THERE COULD BE LEGIONS OF MINIONS JUST WAITING TO STRIKE AND DESTROY EVERYTHING.
HE JUST HAS TO SAY THE WORD AND WE'RE **DOOMED**.

OR NOT. HE MAY BE HARMLESS.
BUT WE WON'T KNOW UNTIL SOMEONE FACES HIM.
UNTIL **I** FACE HIM.

I DON'T WANT PEOPLE TO GET HURT BECAUSE I WAS TOO SCARED TO DO ANYTHING.

I DON'T WANT TO FEEL LIKE A DISAPPOINTMENT.
IF I DECIDE TO DO NOTHING AND SOMETHING BAD HAPPENS, IT'LL BE MY FAULT!

OH, WE WOULD COME UP WITH ANOTHER SOLUTION.

BUT WITH EVERYONE IN HYSTERICS, HOW LONG WOULD THAT TAKE? I DON'T WANT TO RISK IT.
I'D RATHER TRY NOW THAN WAIT UNTIL IT MIGHT BE TOO LATE.

PLUS...
CARROT BELIEVES I CAN DO THIS.

I NEED TO PROVE TO CARROT THAT THEY'RE RIGHT, THAT I AM BRAVE ENOUGH.

AND THAT'S WHY I'M GONNA CONFRONT THAT VAMPIRE AND GET HIM TO LEAVE OR **ELSE!**

WELL, YOUR DECISION TO GO ALREADY PROVES YOU HAVE A LOT OF COURAGE.
BUT I KNOW OF SOME ITEMS THAT MAY AID YOU AND BOOST YOUR BRAVERY.
WOULD YOU LIKE THEM?

OH MY GRAPES! YES!
ANYTHING! PLEASE!
HA
HA
HA

COME WITH ME.

NOW, LET'S SEE.
YOU DEFINITELY WANT TO WAIT UNTIL TOMORROW MORNING TO CONFRONT THIS VAMPIRE.
DO YOU KNOW WHY?

IT'S BECAUSE...

...VAMPIRES DON'T LIKE THE SUN!

CORRECT! IT MAKES THEM WEAK.
THAT WAY, IF YOUR ENCOUNTER TAKES A SOUR TURN, YOU CAN FLEE OUTSIDE.
MOST LIKELY, HE WON'T FOLLOW.

NOW, LOOK FOR A BUSH OR TREE WITH RED BERRIES AND LEAVES LIKE THIS.

OH! I THINK I SAW ONE.

tuft
tuft

screech

TA-DA!

MARVELOUS!

CRACK

LOVELY.

I BELIEVE I HAVE THE REST AT HOME.

COME ALONG.

THERE WE GO.

SNAP

?

NOW, THIS BRANCH IS HAWTHORN.

IT HAS MANY MAGICAL PROPERTIES.

wink

CLAP

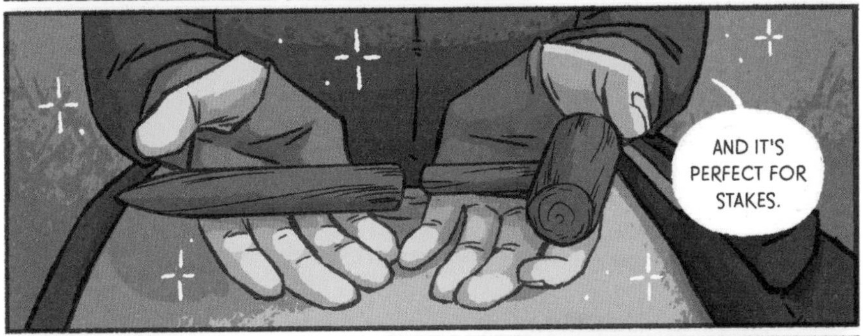
AND IT'S PERFECT FOR STAKES.

VAMPIRES HATE HAWTHORN AS MUCH AS THEY HATE STAKES.
COOL.

FOR SOME
ADDITIONAL
PROTECTION—

THERE.

NOW,
JUST ONE MORE
THING!

IN CASE
YOU NEED A
DISTRACTION
SO YOU CAN
FLEE.

A PERFECT BLEND OF SEEDS AND GRAINS.

IF YOU TOSS THEM ON THE GROUND, THE VAMPIRE WILL BE COMPELLED TO COUNT EVERY SINGLE ONE—

GIVING YOU TIME TO FLEE BEFORE HE DOES YOU ANY HARM.

I KNOW, BUT ONE CAN'T MAKE THIS UP.

MAKES YOU WONDER WHAT OTHER SMALL THINGS CAN STOP A VAMPIRE.

GOT EVERYTHING IN THERE?

YEP!
EXCELLENT!

THE WEATHER HAS GIVEN YOU A NICE SUNNY DAY.
I'LL DO MY BEST TO KEEP ANY CLOUDS AWAY.

RIGHT.

THANK YOU SO MUCH FOR YOUR HELP, WITCH AGNES.
OH, OF COURSE.

flap
flap
AH, THERE YOU ARE.

flap
SOLAS WILL HELP YOU GET TO THE CASTLE AND WILL WAIT TO BRING YOU BACK WHEN ALL IS DONE.

HELLO, SOLAS.

BUT SOLAS WON'T BE THE ONLY ONE.
HUH?

OH, CELERY!

WHAT?!

SINCE THIS WAS YOUR IDEA, I BELIEVE YOU SHOULD GIVE GARLIC SOME ASSISTANCE...

IN CASE THINGS GET HAIRY.

push

HAIRY?!

DON'T WORRY, YOU AREN'T GOING IN UNPROTECTED.

YOU TWO
BEST BE OFF
NOW.

YOU'VE
GOT THIS,
GARLIC.

GOOD LUCK.
kiss

YAY, GARLIC!
YOU CAN DO IT!

YOU'RE GONNA DO GREAT!
WOO!
GET THAT VAMPIRE!

GOOD LUCK, CELERY.

THANKS.

WE'LL BE RIGHT BACK!

READY?
I GUESS.

HERE WE GO.

OKAY, I CAN DO THIS.
I'M BRAVE.
IT'S JUST A VAMPIRE...

...AND I'M GARLIC.
SO I'LL BE SAFE, NO MATTER WHAT.
I CAN TOTALLY DO THIS.

WE'RE GONNA DIE!
WHA--

DON'T SAY THAT! WE'RE GOING TO BE FINE.
NO! WE HAVE TO GO BACK! WE GOTTA--

AAAAH

chapter five

AAAA!!

AAAAAAH

OOF!

WOW.

CHEESE 'N' CHIVES, WE SHOULD NOT BE HERE.

THIS WAS **YOUR** IDEA.

YEAH, BUT I DIDN'T THINK **I** WAS GOING TO BE HERE!
IT WAS SUPPOSED TO BE JUST YOU.

WHY DID WITCH AGNES PICK ME TO GO WITH YOU?
DIDN'T SCALLION AND PUMPKIN SAY THEY'D GO?

SHE **TOLD US** HER REASON.
SHE PICKED YOU BECAUSE YOU MADE EVERYONE PICK ME.

BECAUSE YOU'RE **GARLIC!** EVERYONE KNOWS ABOUT VAMPIRES AND GARLIC!
I'M SURE SOMEONE ELSE WOULD HAVE BROUGHT IT UP IF I HADN'T.

NOW, I'M GOING TO TAKE SOLAS BACK, AND I WILL TELL EVERYONE YOU WERE SO BRAVE THAT YOU MARCHED STRAIGHT INTO THE CASTLE...
...TOLD ME YOU DIDN'T NEED HELP, SO YOU SENT ME HOME.

WHAT?!

OH, COME ON. YOU'LL BE FINE ON YOUR OWN.
AND IF YOU'RE NOT, WELL...

...AT LEAST VAMPIRES AREN'T REALLY KEEN ON CELERY.

SOLAS, PERCH YOURSELF ABOVE THE DOOR!

HEY, WAIT!

perch

WHAT ARE YOU DOING?!

KNOCKING!

PECK THE DOOR THREE TIMES!

KNOCK
KNOCK
KNOCK

ARE YOU **INSANE?**
THE VAMPIRE IS GOING TO HEAR THAT!
THAT'S THE PLAN.

AND THE SECOND THAT DOOR OPENS, I'M GONNA RUSH IN AND GIVE THE VAMPIRE WHAT FOR!

AGAIN!
push

KNOCK
KNOCK
KNOCK

ARE YOU STAYING OR GOING?

I...

I'M OUT OF HERE.

tuft
tuft
tuft

...

AGAIN!

crackle
snap

KNOCK
KNOCK
KNOCK

?

PROBABLY A WOODPECKER...

pop
crackle

KNOCK
KNOCK
KNOCK

KNOCK
clack
KNOCK

KNOCK
KNOCK
clk
clk
KNOCK

flutter
flap

HMM...

Shut
WHAT GAME ARE THEY PLAYING?

VAMPIRE! TAKE HEED!
FOR I AM THE WORLD-FAMOUS VAMPIRE HUNTER, GARLIC!
AND I AM HERE TO VANQUISH YOU!

OH, ARE YOU?

"WORLD-FAMOUS VAMPIRE HUNTER" YOU SAY?
I HAVE ENCOUNTERED THE BEST VAMPIRE HUNTERS IN THE WORLD.
clk

YET I'VE NEVER HEARD OF GARLIC, THE VAMPIRE HUNTER.

OH! I LEAVE NO FOE ALIVE TO WARN OTHERS OF MY SKILL.

BUT I WILL OFFER YOU A DEAL.
LEAVE THIS PLACE AND NEVER RETURN, AND IN EXCHANGE, YOU WON'T FACE MY STAKE!

WHAT IF I SAY NO TO THIS DEAL?
clk
clk

THEN YOU GIVE ME NO CHOICE.
I'LL—
I'LL—
WHO AM I KIDDING? I CAN'T DO THIS.

GO AHEAD AND DO YOUR WORST.

clk
clk
clk

WHAT?

WAIT!

tap
tap
tap

!

WOW...

MR. VAMPIRE—

PLEASE, CALL ME COUNT.

COUNT...

AREN'T YOU GOING TO KILL ME OR SOMETHING?

OF COURSE NOT.

OH...

WELL, I DON'T KNOW WHAT TO DO NOW.
plop

SORRY THIS ISN'T WHAT YOU EXPECTED.

I WAS EXPECTING A SWIFT DEATH, SO I GUESS I'M THANKFUL.

OH, AN ACTION LIKE THAT WOULD'VE VIOLATED THE TERMS OF MY AGREEMENT WITH THE LOCAL VAMPIRE HUNTERS.

OH!

IT'S SOMETHING I DREW UP TO REASSURE FOLKS I MEAN NO HARM.
DOES THIS MEAN YOU DON'T HAVE LEGIONS OF MINIONS WAITING TO EXECUTE YOUR PLAN TO TAKE OVER THE WORLD WITH DARKNESS?

HA HA HA HA HA

OH MY, DEFINITELY NO MINIONS.

HA HA
MINIONS...

I GUESS I USED TO HAVE SOME...
A CENTURY AGO, BUT NOT ANYMORE.

chuckle
WASN'T MEETING THEIR EXPECTATIONS EITHER.

I SIMPLY EXPRESSED INTEREST IN VISITING OTHER LANDS AND SUDDENLY THEY WERE RALLYING TO TAKE OVER THE WORLD.
WORLD DOMINATION?
WHY WOULD ANYONE EVER THINK THAT'D BE A GOOD IDEA?

HONESTLY, IT WAS ALL SUCH A HASSLE.

SO I CAME BACK HERE.
I SIMPLY PLAN TO LIVE OUT MY IMMORTAL LIFE JUST...RELAXING.

I GUESS YOU CAN SAY...
I'M RETIRED.

I SEE...

SO... WHAT DO YOU DO FOR BLOOD?

I'VE ADOPTED A MORE... VEGETARIAN DIET.
ON RARE OCCASIONS, I'LL SAMPLE FROM LOCAL WILDLIFE.
DON'T WORRY, THERE AREN'T ANY VAMPIRE DEER RUNNING AROUND. I JUST NEED A SIP FROM TIME TO TIME.

BUT I MOSTLY STICK TO THIS.
IT'S MY OWN CONCOCTION I'VE DEVELOPED OVER TIME.

A BEETROOT AND TOMATO JUICE BLEND WITH A HINT OF LIME AND A PINCH OF CAYENNE.
TASTES GREAT AND IT'S GOOD FOR THE BLOOD.

I'LL TAKE YOUR WORD FOR IT.

WOULD LOVE TO HAVE A PROPER BLOOD ALTERNATIVE. ALMOST HAD SOMETHING YEARS AGO...
A PROJECT I PLAN TO PICK UP AGAIN.

WAIT...
SO YOU MAKE IT
YOURSELF?
WHERE DO
YOU GET YOUR
PRODUCE?

WELL,
I USED TO POP
INTO MARKETS,
BUT THEN I HAD
AN IDEA.

COME,
LET ME SHOW
YOU.

SO AS YOU CAN SEE, I DECIDED TO START GROWING MY OWN.

THESE PLANTS...
I'VE NEVER SEEN ANY LIKE THEM BEFORE.

WANT A BETTER LOOK?
SURE!
slide

hop

I COLLECTED SPROUTS AND SEEDS ON MY TRAVELS AND I DISCREETLY TOOK CARE OF THEM.
HAD TO KEEP THEM SECRET FROM MY "MINIONS," OF COURSE.

IT'S SO BEAUTIFUL!

THAT WAS WONDERFUL.
YOU HAVE A MIGHTY GREEN THUMB!
THANK YOU!
chuckle

NO, THANK **YOU!**
I JUST REALIZED I HAVE NEVER SEEN SOMEONE ELSE'S GARDEN BEFORE.

YOU GARDEN?

YEP!
WITH THE VEGGIE AND FRUIT FOLK.
THE GARDEN WAS WHERE WE WERE BORN.

IN FACT, I HAVE AN IDEA.
MIND TAKING A WALK?
NOT AT ALL!

THEN FOLLOW ME—
SPIN

SPILL

GASP

OH, GRAPES!
I'M SO SORRY! I DIDN'T MEAN TO--
I-I-I CAN HELP YOU COUNT THEM!

THANK YOU FOR THE OFFER, BUT SADLY I NEED TO COUNT THEM ON MY OWN.

THEN CAN I AT LEAST HELP GATHER THEM FOR YOU?
THAT WOULD BE APPRECIATED, THANK YOU.

ONE...
TWO...
THREE...
tap
tap

chapter six

UGH, WHY AREN'T THEY BACK YET?

IT'S ONLY BEEN A COUPLE HOURS—

EXACTLY! THEY SHOULD'VE BEEN BACK BY NOW!

THEY'RE GOING TO BE FINE.
JUUGH!!

WAIT! I SEE...

...CELERY?

HOLD ON, WHERE ARE GARLIC AND SOLAS?

HI, CELERY!
WELCOME BACK!

CELERY! WHERE'S GARLIC?
DON'T KNOW, DON'T CARE.

WHAT?

WHAT'S THAT SUPPOSED TO MEAN?
THE RAVEN STARTED KNOCKING ON THE DOOR, SO I BOOKED IT.

YOU JUST ABANDONED GARLIC UP THERE?!

YES! BUT SHE'S PROBABLY FINE.
SHE WAS GONNA GO UP THERE BY HERSELF ANYWAY.

I'M SURE SHE'S FINE
SHE'LL BE HERE IN NO TIME.

I'M GONNA HEAD HOME.

CARROT, I THINK SHE--
SHE'S COMING BACK.

WAIT!

LOOK! IT'S SOLAS!
SHE'S BACK!

I DON'T SEE GARLIC ON HIS BACK.
SHE'S THERE.
SHE'S JUST HIDING. SHE—
SHE HAS TO BE!
CARROT, I'M SO SORRY. I...
CARROT! LOOK!
GARLIC?
HI!

SHE DID IT!
SHE'S ALIVE!

GARLIC'S BACK!
SHE DID IT! SHE--
IS NOT ALONE.

SHE'S BRINGING HIM HERE!
WHY?!

ONLY ONE WAY TO FIND OUT...

WHAT DID CARROT SAY?
GARLIC'S BACK?
IS THAT WHAT THEY SAID?
I THINK SO!

CARROT!

I'M SO RELIEVED YOU'RE OKAY.

BUT WHY'S THE VAMPIRE HERE?

'CAUSE HE'S SOMEONE I WANT YOU TO MEET.

CARROT, MEET COUNT.
COUNT, THIS IS CARROT.
AH, I'VE HEARD SO MUCH ABOUT YOU.

AND YOU MUST BE WITCH AGNES.

WHY YES, I AM.
LOVELY TO MEET YOU, THOUGH...
HAVE WE MET BEFORE?

MY MOTHER, PERHAPS.
SHE WAS THE HEAD WITCH OF THE VALLEY BEFORE I TOOK THE ROLE.

AH, YES! SHE WAS A GREAT HELP TO ME LONG, LONG AGO.

WE WERE CLOSE TO MAKING A BLOOD SUBSTITUTE FOR ME.
PERHAPS YOU COULD HELP ME?
OF COURSE.
ahem
GARLIC, WOULD YOU PLEASE TELL US WHY YOU'VE BROUGHT COUNT HERE?
OH, YES!
EVERYONE, I'D LIKE YOU TO MEET COUNT.
HE IS GOING TO START HELPING US IN THE GARDEN.

WHAT?
A **VAMPIRE** IN THE **GARDEN!**
OH MY!

I KNOW, I KNOW...
BUT TRUST ME, HE MEANS NO HARM.
INDEED.
AND HE WANTS TO LEARN MORE ABOUT GARDENING.

PLUS YOU HAVE TO SEE HIS GARDEN.
IT'S GORGEOUS, WITH SO MANY PLANTS I'VE NEVER SEEN BEFORE!

YES, YOU ARE ALL MORE THAN WELCOME TO VISIT.

HMM, I DON'T KNOW.
HE SEEMS NICE.
BUT HOW DO WE KNOW SOMETHING BAD WON'T HAPPEN?

YOU KNOW WHAT?

I WOULD LOVE SOME HELP FROM A NEW FRIEND.

IT'D BE MY PLEASURE.

IT'S NICE TO MEET YOU, COUNT.

WELCOME!

HEY, THERE!

HELLO!

HAPPY TO MEET YOU!

ahem

sigh

NICE TO
MEET YOU...

AH!

I GUESS I HAVE YOU TO THANK FOR GARLIC'S LITTLE VISIT TO MY CASTLE.

IT'S A SHAME YOU FLED, THOUGH. I'M SURE YOU FEEL TERRIBLE FOR DOING THAT.

YEP, SURE DO!
HA
HA

GOODBYE!
IT WAS NICE TO MEET YOU!
SEE YOU LATER!

poof

WHAT!

shrug

the end

RECORD YOUR THOUGHTS HERE & LOCK 'EM UP. OPERATIVES OF TOMORROW WILL NEED YOUR GENIUS TO SURVIVE.
DRAGON
2022
HE-24
TA2

POW!
BOOM!
BAM
CRASH
POOF!
SNAP!

DUDE
DIARY
BOOM!
WRITE! DRAW!
DESTROY!

DUDE DIARY BOOM!

CREATED BY
MICKEY
AND
CHERYL
GILL

FLEEING THE IMMINENT EXPLOSION OF THE PLANET WE ARE VISITING ...

FINE print
PUBLISHING

Fine Print Publishing Company
P.O. Box 916401
Longwood, Florida 32791-6401

Created in the U.S.A. & Printed in China
This book is printed on acid-free paper.

ISBN 978-1-892951-76-2

2 3 5 7 9 10 8 6 4 1

thedudebook.com

PROPERTY OF:

YOUR BEST FRIEND IS AN ALIEN. PLUS YOU HAVE THE CHANCE TO CREATE A BRO FOR FRANKENSTEIN'S MONSTER, DESIGN THE OLYMPICS OF TOMORROW, USE A CLONING MACHINE, AND TOSS ANNOYING THINGS INTO A GINORMOUS SPIDER WEB.

AND DUDE, THAT'S JUST FOR STARTERS.

GET BUSY, BRO.

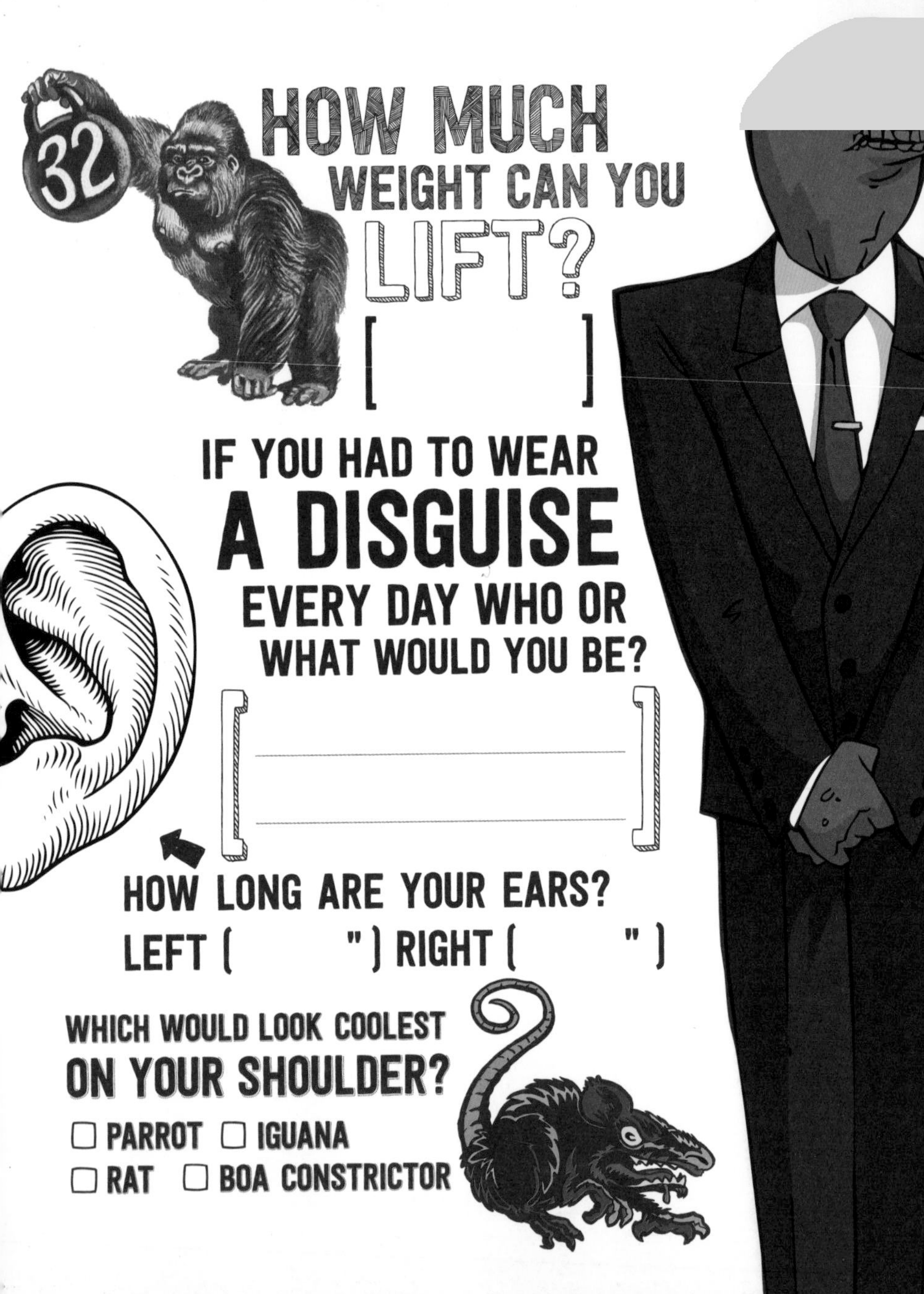
32
HOW MUCH
WEIGHT CAN YOU
LIFT?
[ ]
IF YOU HAD TO WEAR
A DISGUISE
EVERY DAY WHO OR
WHAT WOULD YOU BE?
[ ]
HOW LONG ARE YOUR EARS?
LEFT (") RIGHT (")
WHICH WOULD LOOK COOLEST
ON YOUR SHOULDER?
☐ PARROT ☐ IGUANA
☐ RAT ☐ BOA CONSTRICTOR

WHICH WOULD BE AH-MAZING TO BE IN CONTROL OF AT SCHOOL?

- ☐ LUNCH MENU
- ☐ P.E.
- ☐ HIRING TEACHERS
- ☐ OTHER? ________________

WHICH SONG SHOULD PLAY EVERY TIME YOU ENTER A ROOM?

[ ]

HAS A TIC EVER BURROWED UNDER YOUR SKIN?

- ☐ OF COURSE
- ☐ AHHH! NO!

ON A SCALE OF 1-10, HOW DANGEROUS R U?

1 2 3 4 5 6 7 8 9 10 DANGER! DANGER! DANGER!

HOW MANY POUNDS OF SNOT DO YOU THINK YOU PRODUCE A YEAR?

{ }

HAVE YOU EVER THOUGHT SO HARD IT MADE YOUR BRAIN HURT?

- YES
- NO

YOU ACCIDENTALLY SEE YOUR BEST BUD TURNING INTO AN ALIEN! AHHH!!!

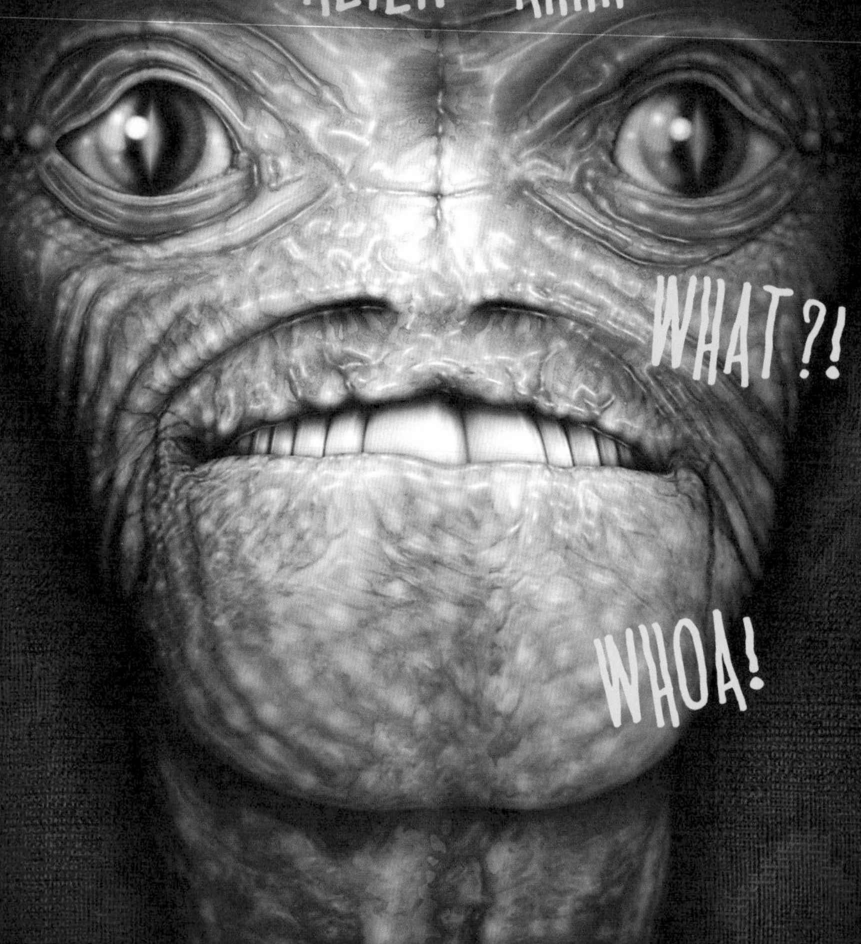

HE DOESN'T KNOW YOU KNOW HIS SECRET. HOW WILL YOU HANDLE IT?

1ST THING YOU'LL DO?

THEN WHAT?

WHAT SHOULD BE BANNED FROM SCHOOL?

That weird
hamburger meat.
Homework.

THE DESTR
HAS BEEN REPROGRAMMED TO DO GOOD, AND YOU'RE THE BOSS OF HIM!

FOR THE GOOD OF ALL MANKIND, WHAT TERRIBLE THINGS WILL YOU ORDER HIM TO

DESTROY?

CLAWS-
TROPHOBIC
WHAT ARE
THE MOST FRIGHTENING
CREATURES WITH CLAWS?

a werewolf because
if it gets really close to
you it

IF YOU POSTED A SMELLFIE OF YOU RIGHT NOW WHAT WOULD IT REEK OF?

Ripe sweat from P.E.

1. Me and Aidyn

2. me

3. me and my dog

4. me and my bunny

5. me and my family

WOULD YOU RATHER

- [ ] FLOSS AN ALLIGATOR'S **TEETH**
- [x] PUT TINY SHOES ON A **BLACK** WIDOW SPIDER
- [ ] TAKE A HOT AIR BALLOON RID WITH A **COBRA?**

WHAT WOULD BE YOUR PLAN? HOW WOULD YOU AVOID THE BITE?

My plan wauld be swim with it take tape with me and tape its moufh shut.

STUFF THAT DRIVES PEOPLE CRAZY!

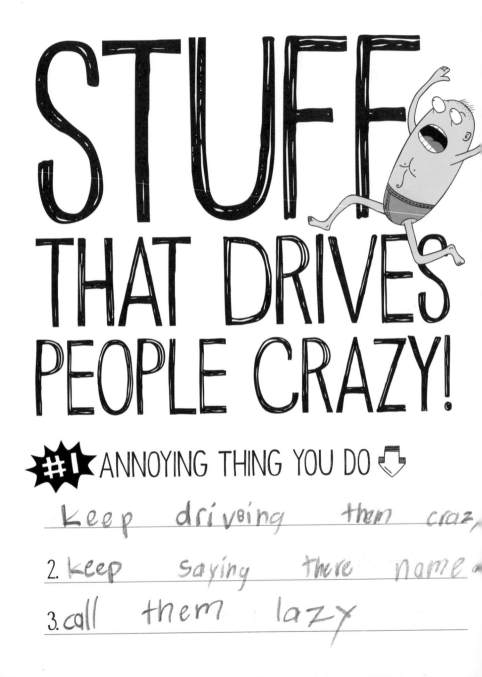

Keep driving them crazy

2. keep saying there name

3. call them lazy

OU DO

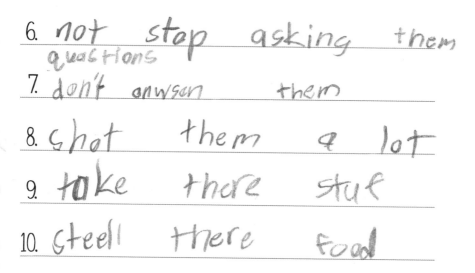

4. make nozese
5. be noze
6. not stop asking them quastions
7. don't anwsen them
8. shot them a lot
9. take there stuf
10. steell there food

CREATE AN AWESOME NEW! CEREAL

WHAT'S THE FLAVOR?

WHAT'S THE SHAPE?

WHAT'S ITS COOL NAME?

DESIGN THE BOX

Fraunt

18

18

18

back

18

18

Manning

18

Why did peyton Manning die.

WOULD YOU RATHER HAVE A
KILLER
☐ WHALE ☐ BEE ☐ KOI?
WHAT WOULD BE
RIDUNKULOUS
TO MORPH INTO?
FAVORITE ACTION
MOVIE STAR?

WHICH IS **SCARIEST?**

- ☐ WAKING A HYBERNATING BEAR
- ☐ TRIPPING OVER A RATTLESNAKE
- ☐ SURFING INTO A STINGRAY

WHAT WOULD YOU BE WILLING TO TRY?

- ☐ ESCARGOT (A.K.A. SNAILS, DUDE!)
- ☐ CAVIAR (FANCY WORD FOR FISH EGGS)
- ☐ SASHIMI (RAW FISH)

LONGEST YOU'VE GONE WEARING THE SAME PAIR OF UNDERWEAR? ☐

☐ MIMES ☐ CLOWNS ☐ VENTRILOQUISTS' DUMMIES

ARE THE CREEPIEST!

DO YOU KNOW WHAT **GIZZARDS** ARE? ☐ YES ☐ NO

CAN YOU THINK OF ANY WORSE JOBS?

**ASK YOURSELF. ASK YOUR FRIENDS.
ASK YOUR STINKY DOG.**

Which is SUPER FOUL?

- PROFESSIONAL CLOGGED TOILET PLUNGER
- DOG PARK POOPER SCOOPER PICKER-UPPER
- MOUTHWASH COMPANY HALITOSIS SNIFFER
- ZOO CAGE LINER CHANGER
- DEODORANT COMPANY SWEATY ARMPIT SMELLER
- FERTILIZER COMPANY CHICKEN AND COW MANURE COLLECTOR

That's baaad breath!

USTING JOB EVER?!!

MASH UP SOME EXTINCT ANIMALS WITH SOME THAT EXIST TODAY

WOOLLY MAMMOTH
DODO BIRD
TYRANNOSAURUS REX
TRICERATOPS
PTERODACTYL
SABER-TOOTHED TIGER
VELOCIRAPTOR
MASTODON

INSANE MASH-UP IDEAS

YOUR BRO-GADE

(A.K.A. BRIGADE OF BROTHERS)

IS REQUIRED TO WEAR UNIFORMS.

YOU GET TO DESIGN THEM!

COME UP WITH A NAME FOR YOUR POSSE WHILE YOU'RE AT IT.

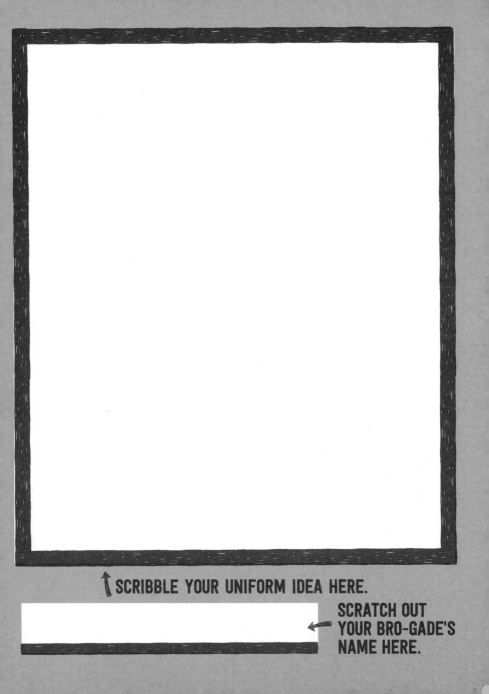

SCRIBBLE YOUR UNIFORM IDEA HERE.

SCRATCH OUT YOUR BRO-GADE'S NAME HERE.

IF YOU WERE AS **FAST** AS THE **FLASH** WHAT WOULD YOU DO WITH YOUR UNBELIEVABLE ABILITY?

REMEMBER, HE DOES EVERYTHING FAST!

GO BIG or GO Home!

WHAT WOULD BE WAY BETTER IF IT WERE WAY BIGGER?

1.
2.
3.
4.
5.
6.
7.
8.
9.
10.

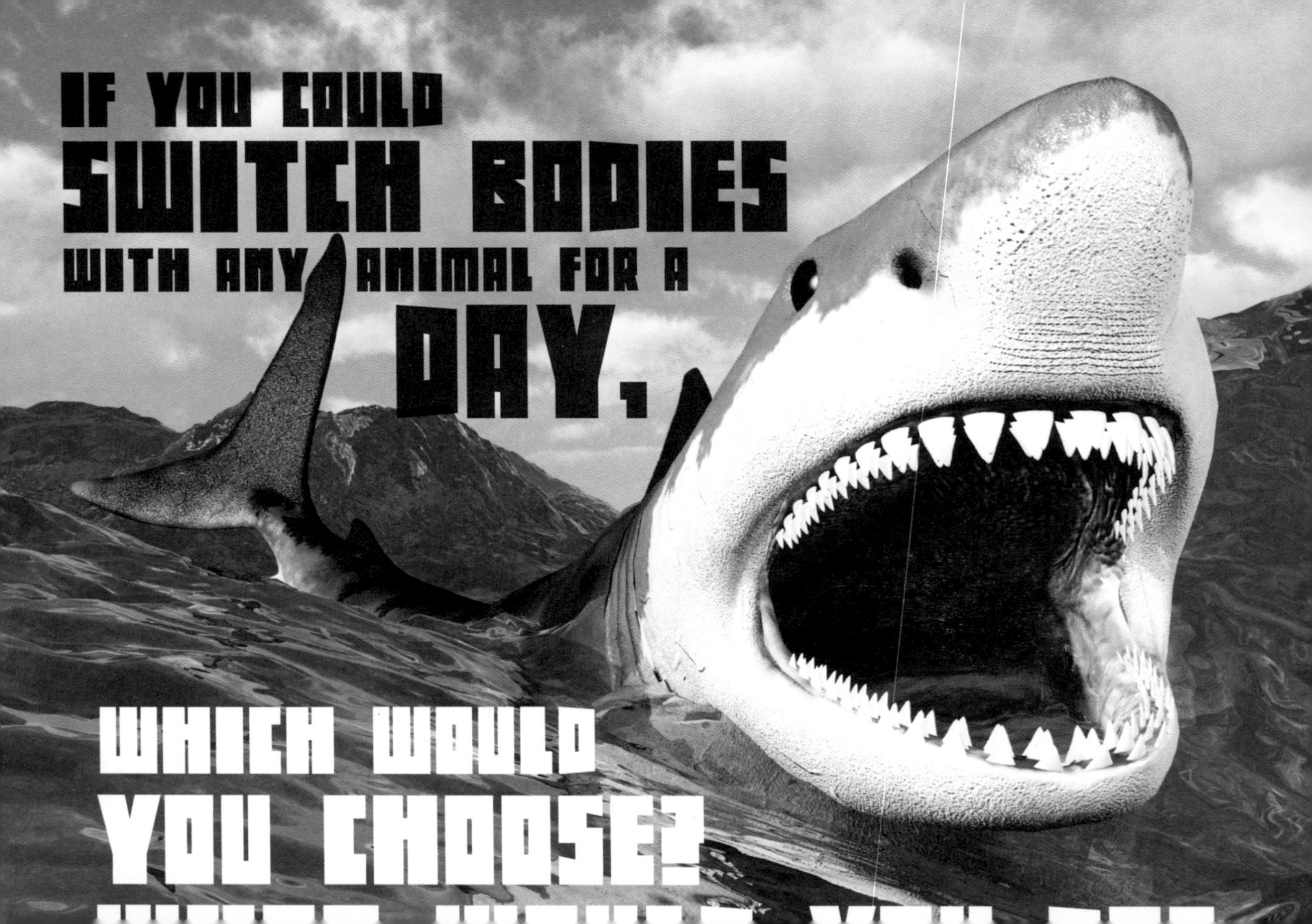
IF YOU COULD
SWITCH BODIES
WITH ANY ANIMAL FOR A
DAY,
WHICH WOULD
YOU CHOOSE?

FINISH THESE CRAZY EXCUSES

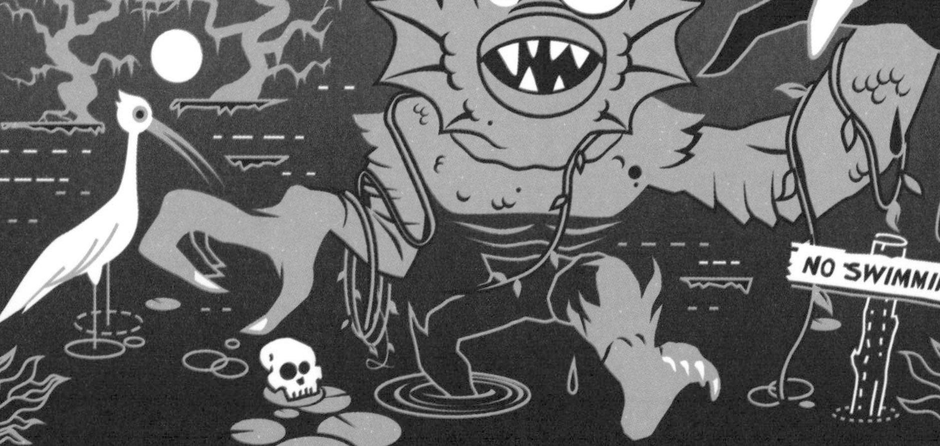

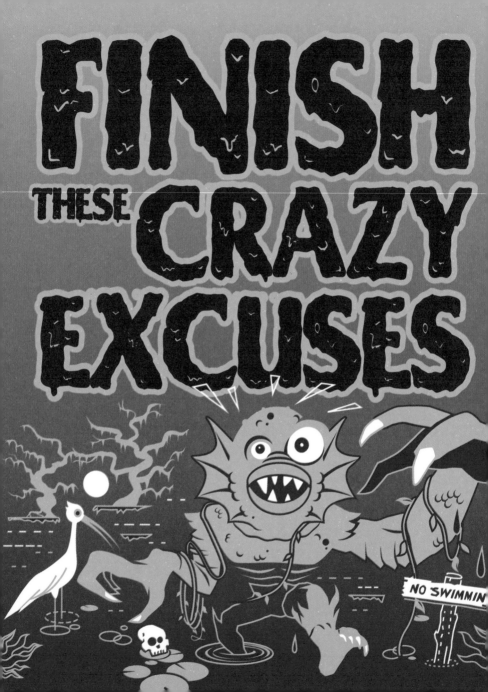

I'm sorry I'm late, but my elephant ______________________

____

I was getting ready to take the garbage out and

then this ______________________________________

______________________________________ in my room.

The **SWAMP THING** ______________________________

____

and that's how the mac 'n' cheese ended up on the ceiling.

I couldn't ______________________________________

because I was busy _______________________________

____________________ with the aliens in the backyard.

A giant, man-eating hamburger _____________________

____

____

so I didn't get my homework done.

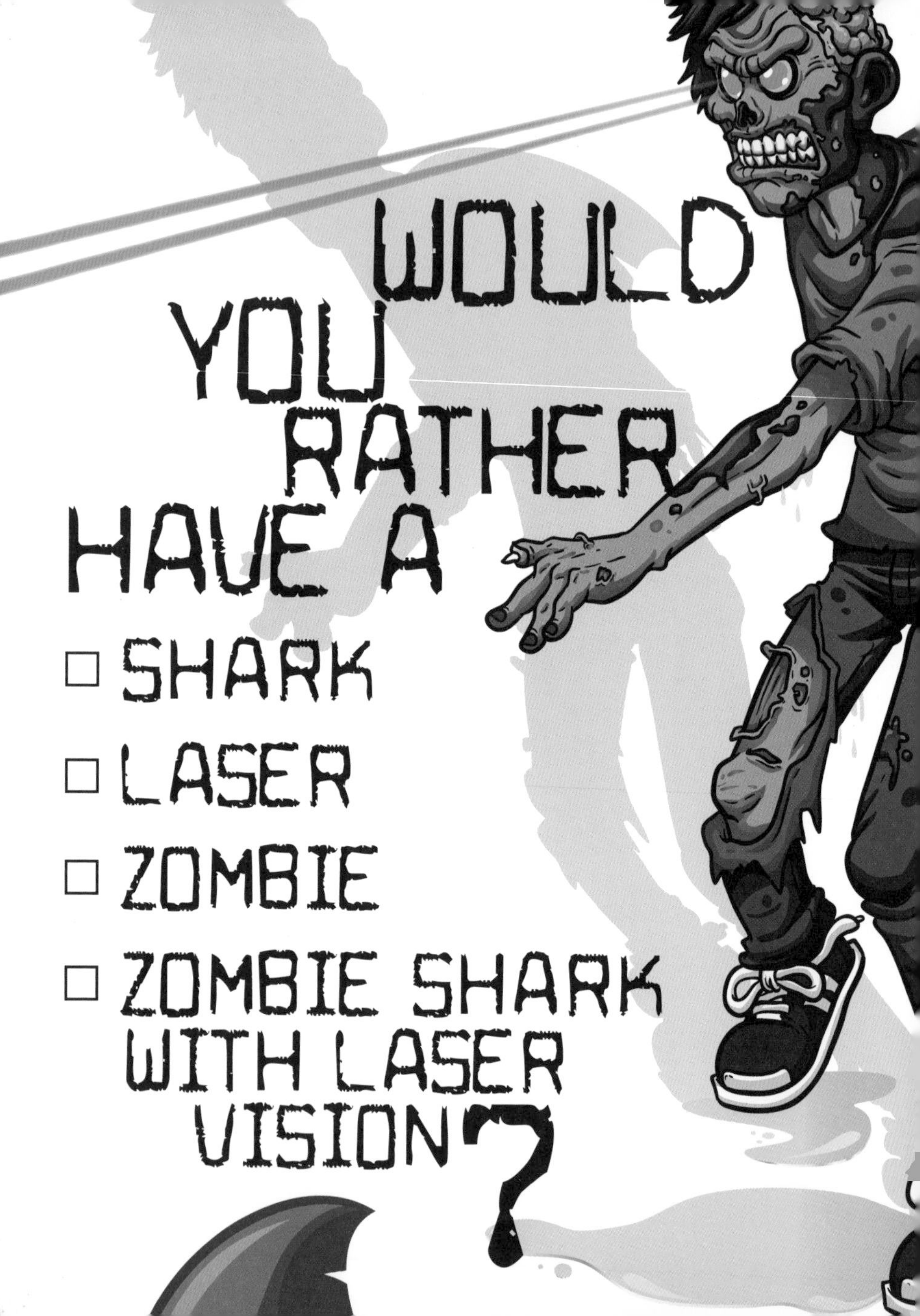
WOULD YOU RATHER HAVE A
☐ SHARK
☐ LASER
☐ ZOMBIE
☐ ZOMBIE SHARK WITH LASER VISION?

WHAT OUTRAGEOUS THINGS WOULD YOU DO WITH IT?

SO YOU HAV
TO STAY IN
YOUR ROOM
FOR ONE WEE
WHAT DO YOU NEE
TO KEEP COMFORTAB

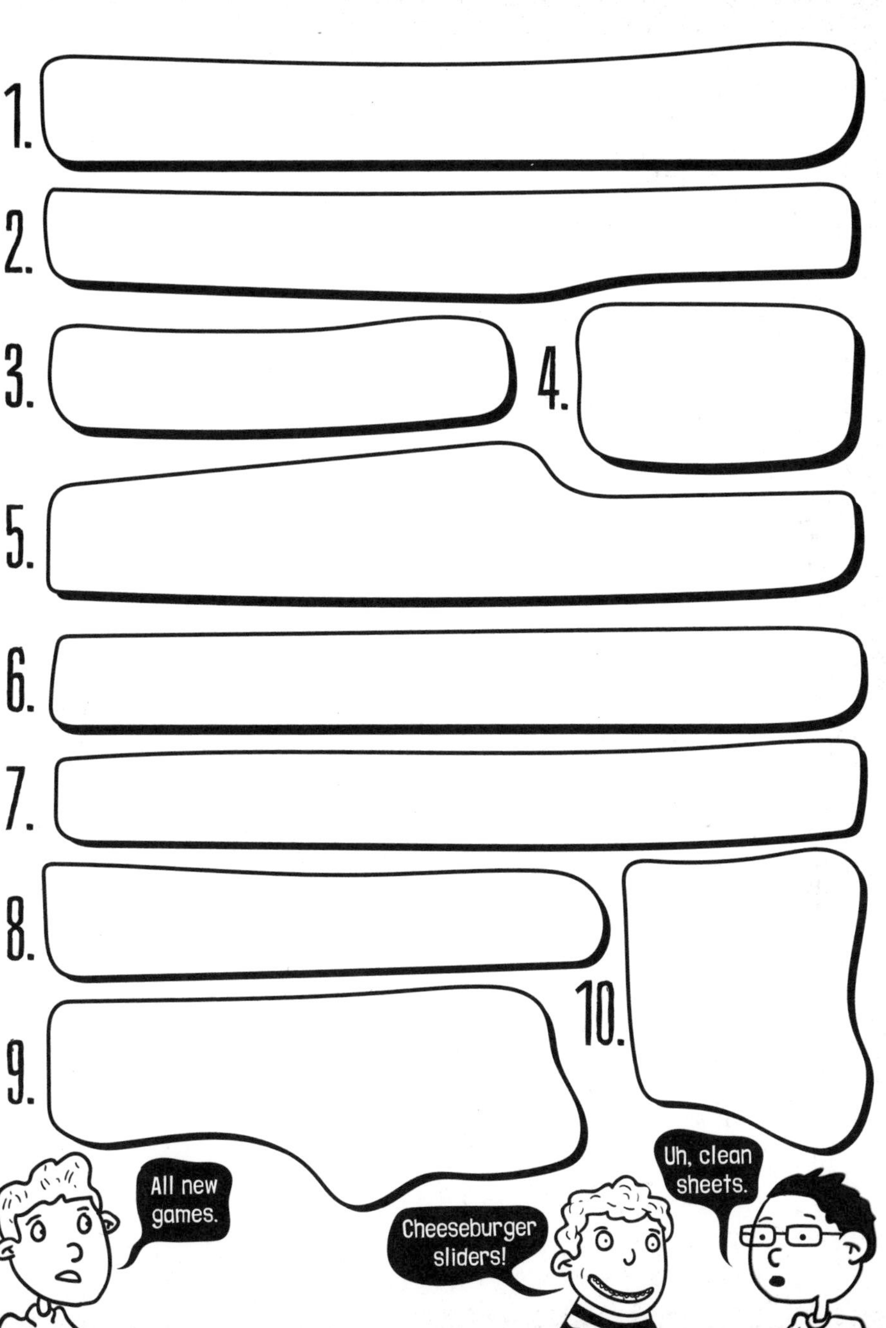
1.
2.
3.
4.
5.
6.
7.
8.
9.
10.
All new games.
Cheeseburger sliders!
Uh, clean sheets.

MEATBALLS
THEY'RE MEAT IN THE SHAPE OF BALLS.
WHAT'S NOT TO LOVE?

WHAT ELSE WOULD BE AWESOME IN THE SHAPE OF A BALL?

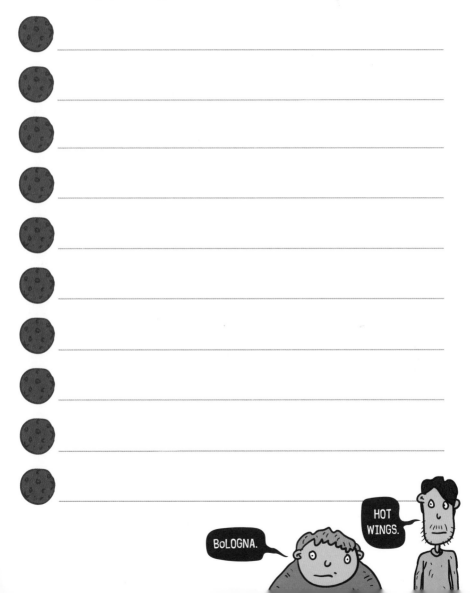

FOOD YOU WOULD STILL EAT IF THERE WERE A 1 IN 10 CHANCE THAT IT MIGHT BITE BACK?

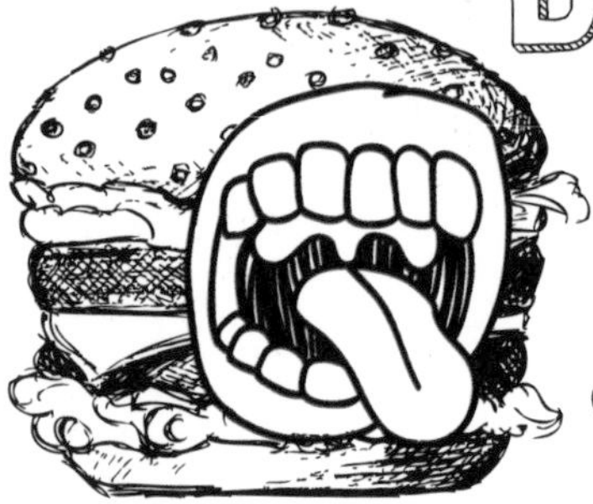

{ ______________________ }

FOUNTAIN OF

☐ CHOCOLATE

☐ CHEESE

☐ OTHER? ______________

WOULD YOU RATHER BE STUCK IN A

☐ BARN FULL OF GASSY COWS

☐ HABITAT OF HIPPOS WITH BAD BREATH

☐ ROOM FULL OF GORILLAS WITH KILLER B.O.?

SOMETHING GIRLS ⇨ LOVE THAT'S REALLY STUPID?

[______________________

______________________]

A PHASER THAT ALSO SHOOTS

☐ PIZZA ROLLS ☐ POTATO SKINS ☐ CHICKEN WINGS?

WOULD YOU RATHER HAVE YOUR OWN ...

☐ PIRATE SHIP
☐ BLIMP
☐ SUBMARINE?

WHAT'S SOMETHING YOU LIKE THAT'S PRETTY RIDICULOUS?

[ ]

FACE PLANT INTO A

☐ CAKE
☐ DONUT
☐ PIE?

BEST FRIEND TO BE WITH IF YOU WERE TRYING TO ESCAPE FROM AN EVIL VILLAIN WHO HAD KIDNAPPED YOU AND SUSPENDED YOU ABOVE A SHARK-INFESTED POOL?

{ }

AWESOME SAUCE

SAUCES, DIPS, & CONDIMENTS THAT ROCK!

SAUCES, DIPS, & CONDIMENTS THAT MAKE YOU

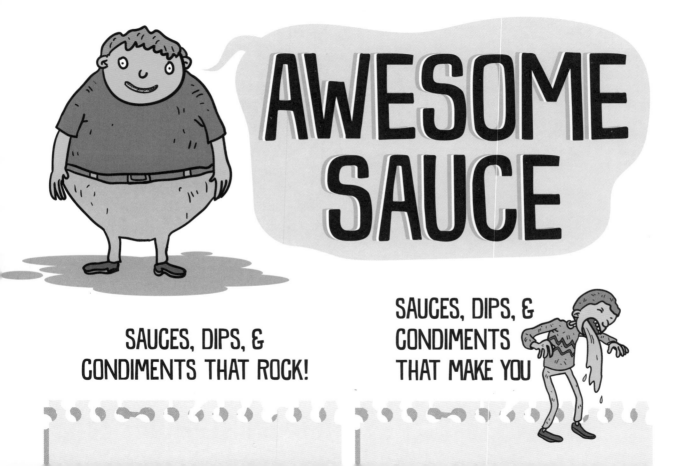

YOU NEED AN INSANELY
SMART
SMART-
PHONE.
WHAT
CRAZY
FEATURES
SHOULD IT HAVE?

UH, A POCKET KNIFE?
IT SHOULD DISPENSE KIBBLE.
I WANT IT TO READ MY GERBIL'S MIND.

FRANK 'N'

FRANKENSTEIN'S MONSTER NEEDS
SOMEONE TO HANG WITH.

WHAT WILL YOU USE TO PIECE TOGETHER
A BEASTY BRO FOR HIM?

LIST STUFF TO MAKE FRANKENSTEIN'S MONSTER 2.

1. ______________________

2. ______________________

3. ______________________

4. ______________________

5. ______________________

6. ______________________

7. ______________________

8. ______________________

9. ______________________

10. ______________________

IEND'S MONSTER

DRAW YOUR CREATION HERE.

MAKE YOUR NAME STAND FOR SOMETHING

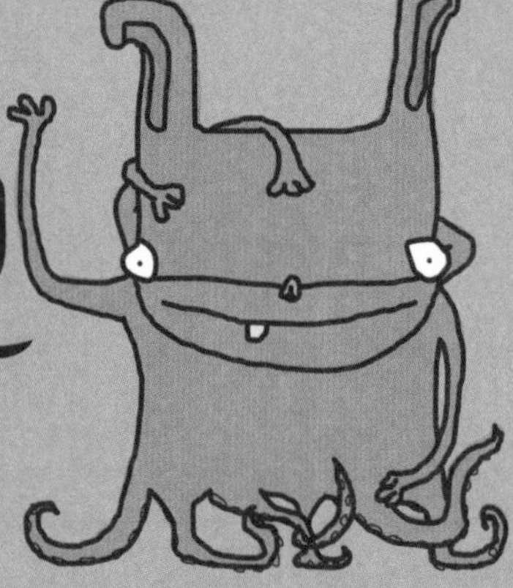

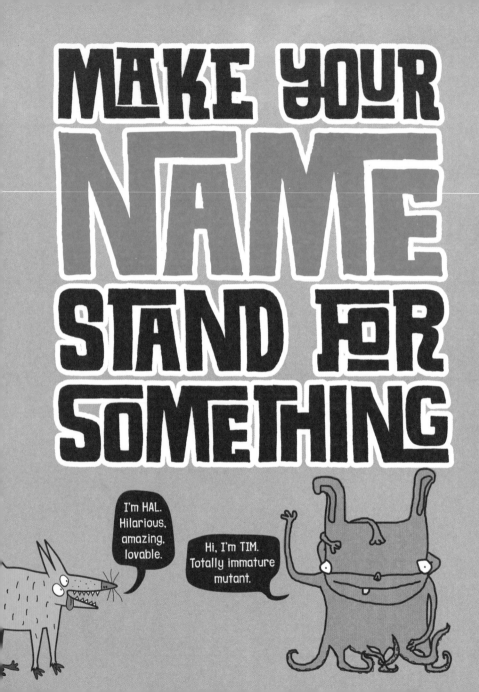

MAKE EACH LETTER IN YOUR NAME STAND FOR A WORD THAT BEGINS WITH THE SAME LETTER— A WORD THAT DESCRIBES YOU OR ONE YOU JUST LIKE.

LETTER IN YOUR NAME	WORD IT STANDS FOR
☐	____________________
☐	____________________
☐	____________________
☐	____________________
☐	____________________
☐	____________________
☐	____________________
☐	____________________
☐	____________________

I
COULD
TOTALLY
SET THE
WORLD RE

1.	
2.	
3.	
4.	
5.	

ORD FOR

YOU ARE THE PROUD OWNER OF A CLONING MACHINE

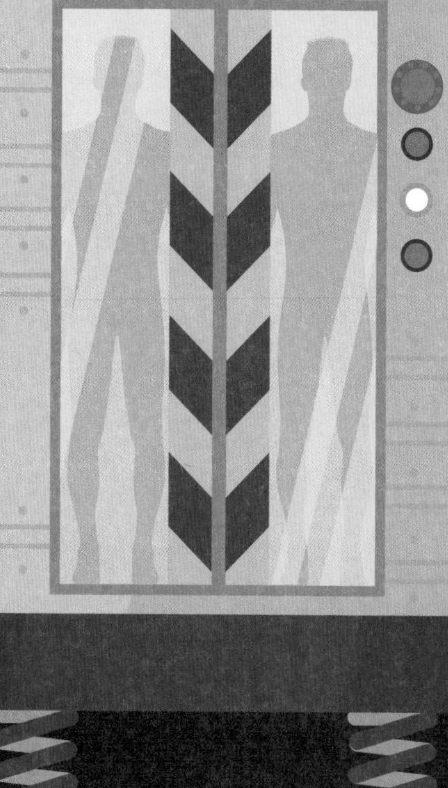

WHAT WILL YOU CLONE?

1.

2.

3.

4.

5.

6.

7.

8.

9.

10.

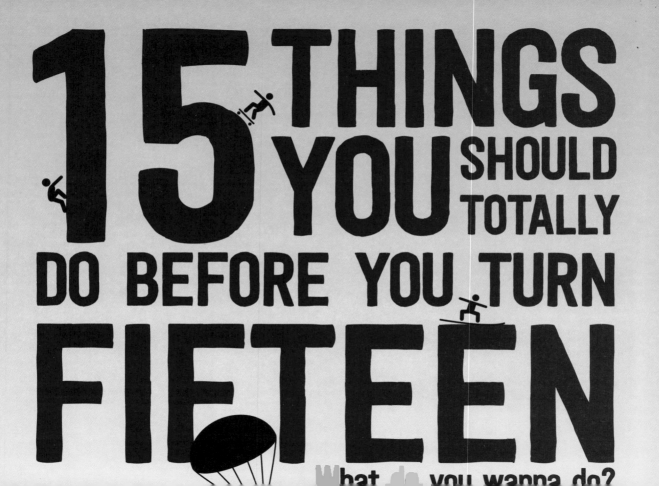

15 THINGS YOU SHOULD TOTALLY DO BEFORE YOU TURN FIFTEEN

What do you wanna do?

RUNNING LOW
ON CHEESE
CURLS, SIR.
SNACKS

YOU HAVE A PERSONAL ROBO-VENDING MACHINE-BOT. IT FOLLOWS YOU EVERYWHERE. WHAT WILL YOU FILL IT WITH?

A1	A2
B1	B2
C1	C2
D1	D2
E1	E2
F1	F2
G1	G2
H1	H2

IF YOU WERE GUARANTEED THAT YOU WOULD ABSOLUTELY NOT GET HURT WHAT

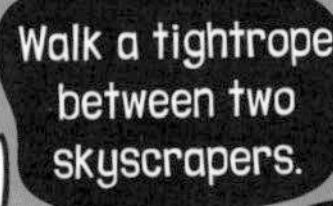

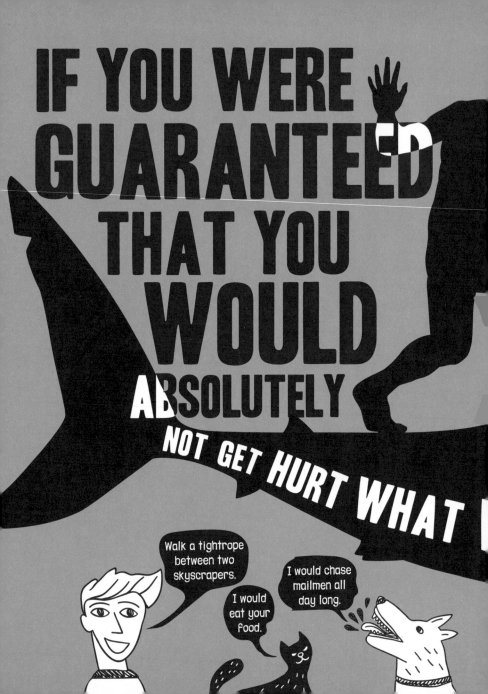

1. ______________________

2. ______________________

3. ______________________

4. ______________________

5. ______________________

ULD YOU TRY?

PROPS TO YOU!
Uh, I can shoot a spitball across my room.
We pull pranks and blame it on our other triplet.

WHAT AWESOME FEATS CAN YOU DO?

I can destroy a pillow in less than a minute.

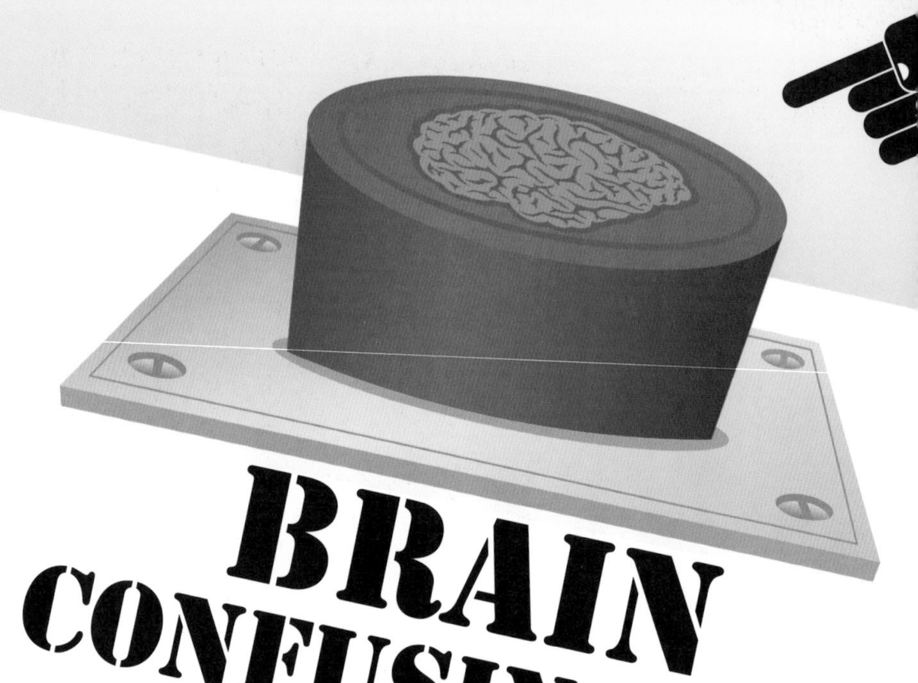

BRAIN CONFUSINATOR 5000

DELUXE

WITH JUST A TOUCH OF THIS BUTTON YOU CAN CONTROL PEOPLE'S MINDS. HOW WOULD YOU USE THE BRAIN CONFUSINATOR 5000 DELUXE?

THESE ARE
TERRORIZING
YOUR 'HOOD

CREATE AN URBAN LEGEND

GIVE 'EM A NAME

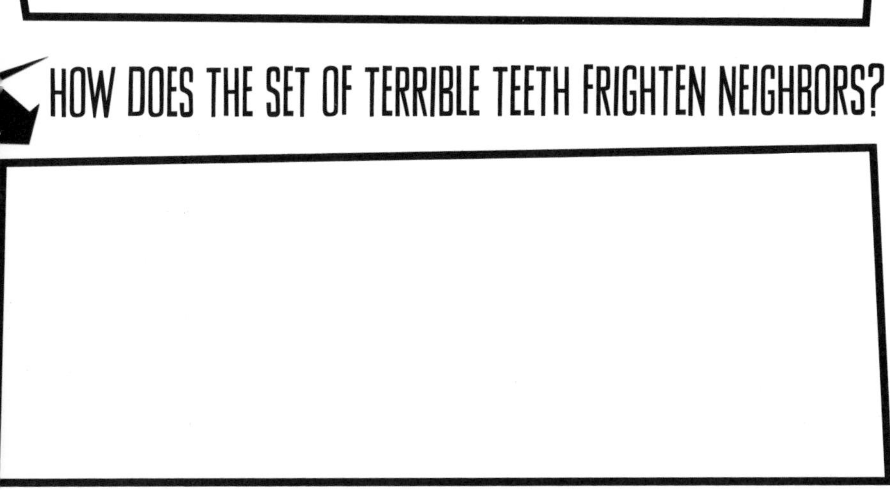

HOW DOES THE SET OF TERRIBLE TEETH FRIGHTEN NEIGHBORS?

HOW WILL **YOU** STOP THE MOUTHY MENACE?

DOWNLOAD YOUR BRAIN

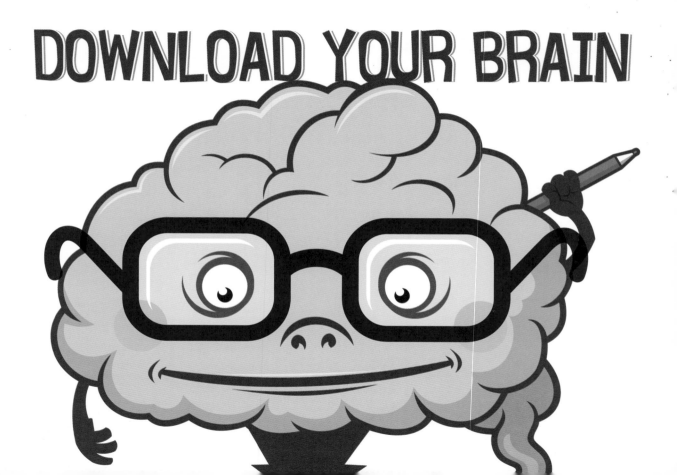

WHAT SUPER IMPORTANT INFORMATION DO YOU KEEP IN YOUR HEAD?

YOU THINK ABOUT A LOT?

OR, WHAT'S FILLING YOUR HEAD CAVITY RIGHT NOW?

I can name all the quarterbacks in the NFL.

I have memorized the location of my fave fire hydrants.

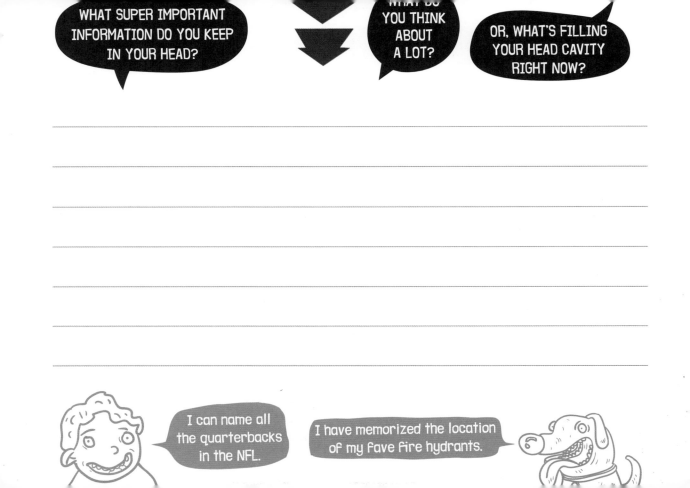

CHOOSE 3 NUMBERS

1 2 3 4 5

6 7 8 9 10

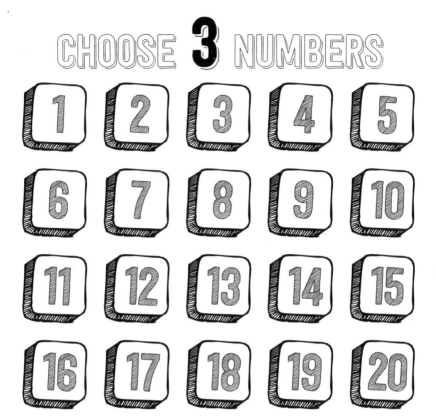

11 12 13 14 15

16 17 18 19 20

TURN THE BOOK UPSIDE DOWN AND FIND OUT WHAT EACH NUMBER STANDS FOR.

1. Orangutan 2. Vat of Jello 3. Helicopter 4. Bounce House 5. Kangaroo
6. Porta-Potty 7. Box of Pizza Pockets 8. School of Dancing Fish
9. Piece of Talking Blubber 10. Ghost of Bulging Biceps
11. Group of Eyeballs on the Loose 12. Giant Pumpkin Pie 13. Flying Buffalo
14. Llama 15. Can of Cheez Whiz 16. Hockey Team 17. Dino-Chicken
18. Crate of Bottle Rockets 19. Time Machine 20. Box of Refried Beans

NOW FILL IN THE BLANKS WITH YOUR THREE CHOICES

YOUR FAMILY DISCOVERS A(N) ____________________

A(N) ____________________, AND A(N) ____________________

IN YOUR BEDROOM. HOW DO YOU EXPLAIN?

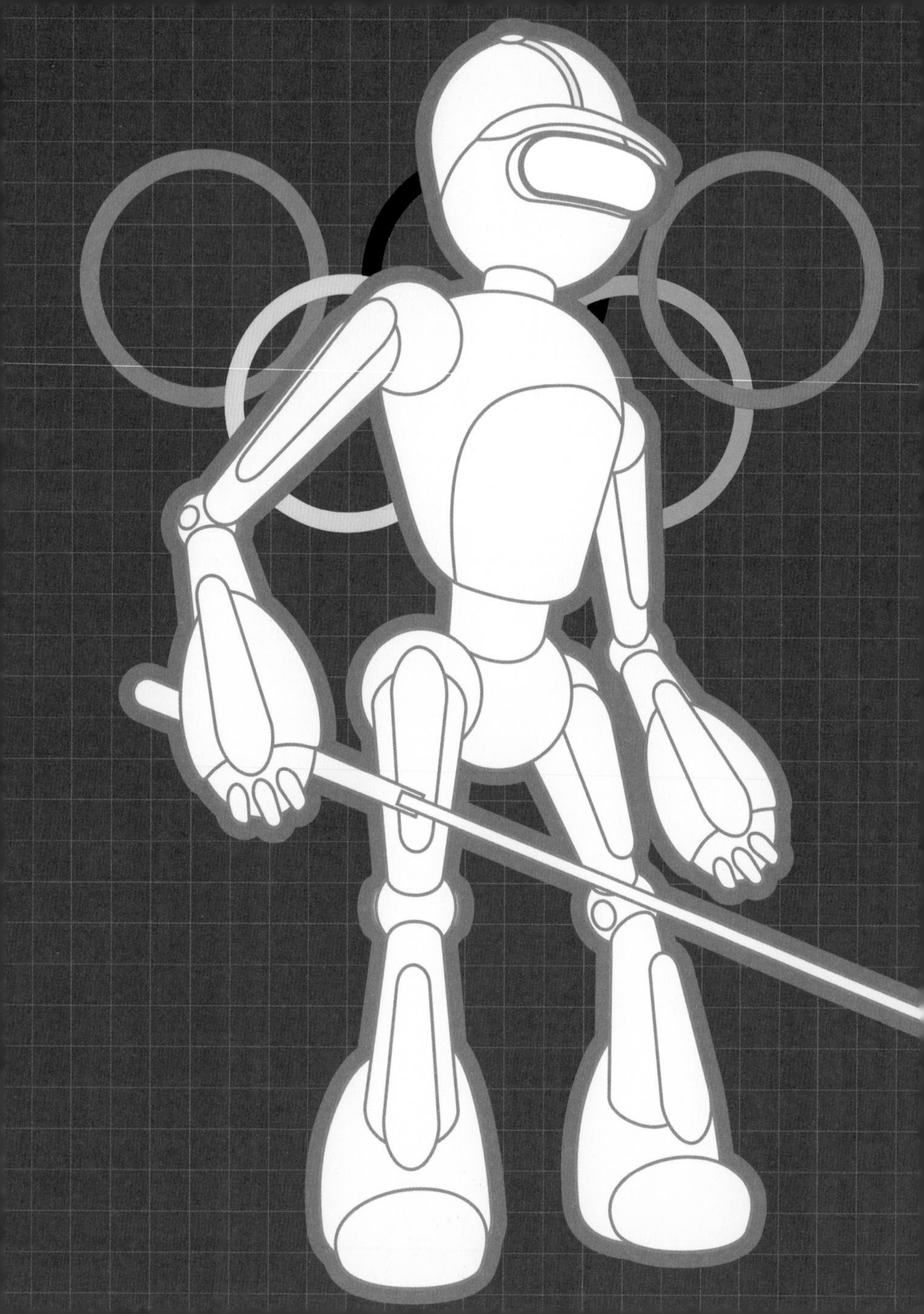

BRAINSTORM SOME MIND-BLOWING SPORTS FOR THE OLYMPICS OF THE DISTANT FUTURE.

HOVER SKATE-BOARD TENNIS.

JETPACK SPEED SKATING.

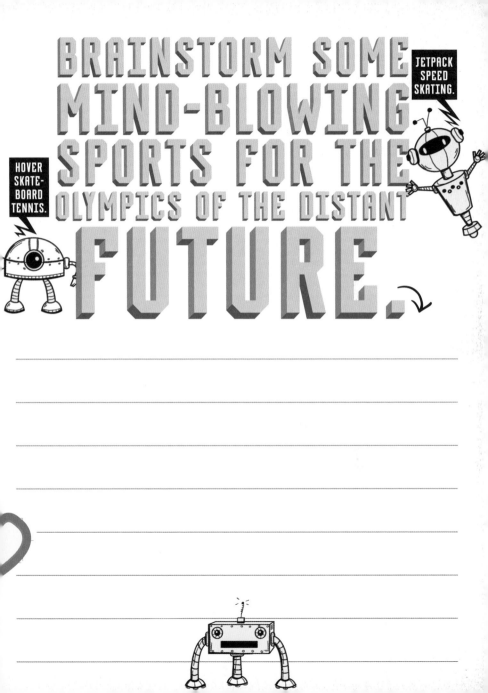

YOU SHOULD DONATE ALL YOUR MONEY TO ME.

PUT ME DOWN. I SMELL LIKE A DEAD FISH.

DON'T MAKE KIDS DO CHORES.

DON'T MAKE SHOWERS MANDATORY FOR DUDES.

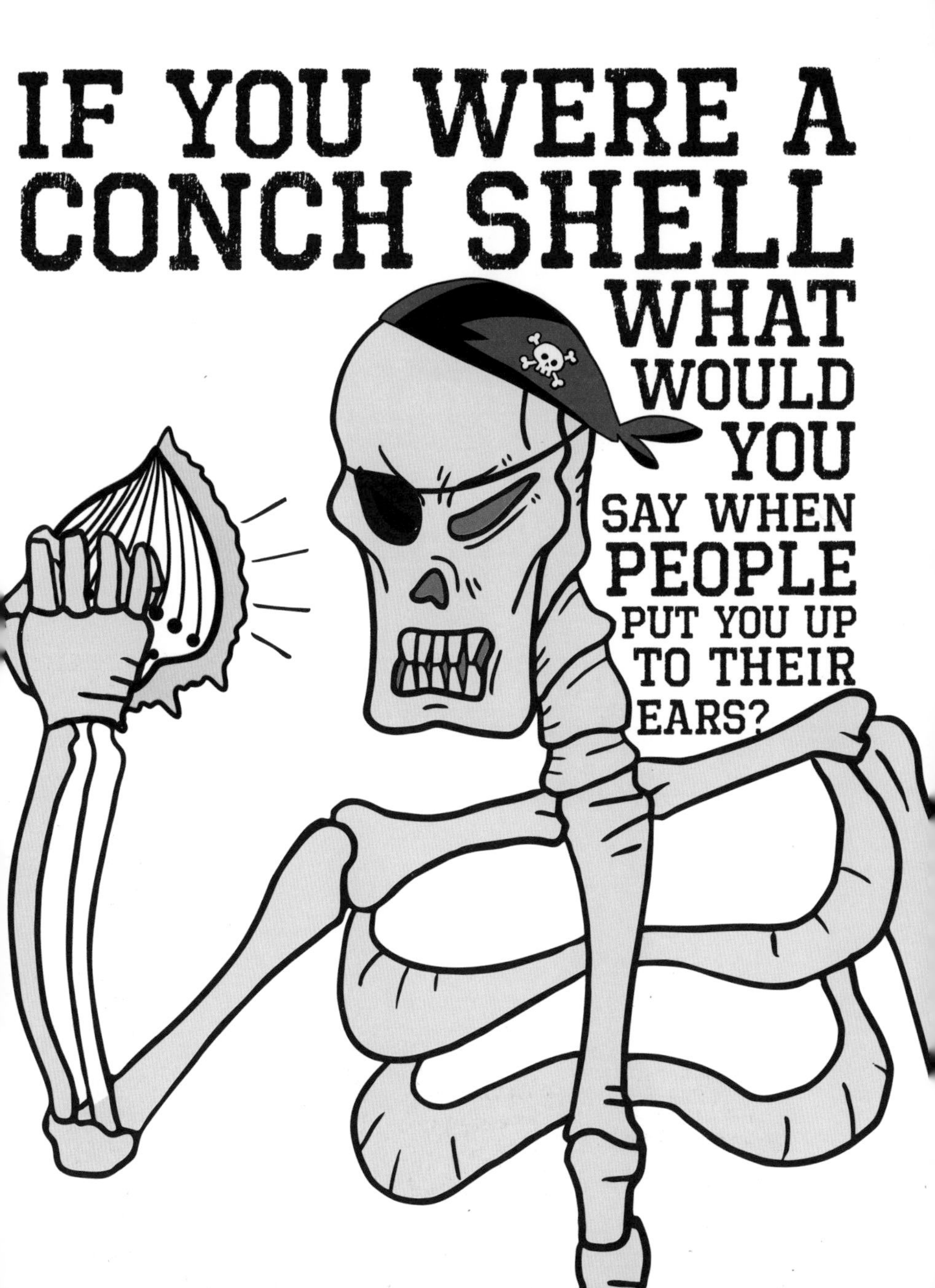
IF YOU WERE A
CONCH SHELL
WHAT
WOULD
YOU
SAY WHEN
PEOPLE
PUT YOU UP
TO THEIR
EARS?

MUTANT MEN

GIVE LIFE TO SOME RIDUNKULOUS ANIMAL-MAN COMBOS.

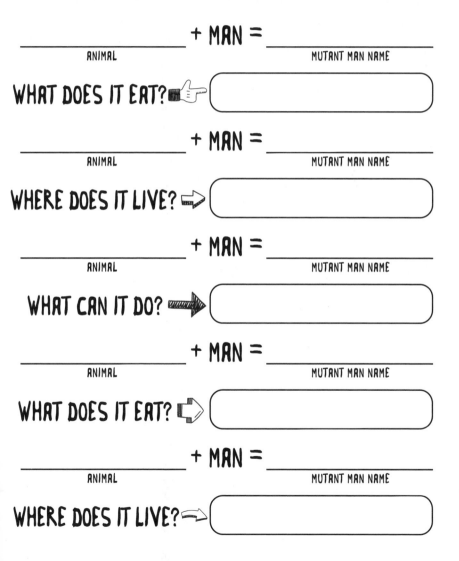

________________ + MAN = ________________
ANIMAL MUTANT MAN NAME

WHAT DOES IT EAT?

________________ + MAN = ________________
ANIMAL MUTANT MAN NAME

WHERE DOES IT LIVE?

________________ + MAN = ________________
ANIMAL MUTANT MAN NAME

WHAT CAN IT DO?

________________ + MAN = ________________
ANIMAL MUTANT MAN NAME

WHAT DOES IT EAT?

________________ + MAN = ________________
ANIMAL MUTANT MAN NAME

WHERE DOES IT LIVE?

SCIENTISTS CAN NOW

SHRINK A

SUBMARINE (AND ITS CREW)

TO A TINY SIZE THAT CAN FIT INSIDE A HUMAN BODY.

YOU'VE BEEN RECRUITED BY THE SCIENTISTS TO BE PART OF THE

HUMAN INNARDS EXPLORATION TEAM

WHERE DO YOU WANT TO GO?

BEHIND AN EYEBALL,
SMALL INTESTINES,
LARGE INTESTINES ...

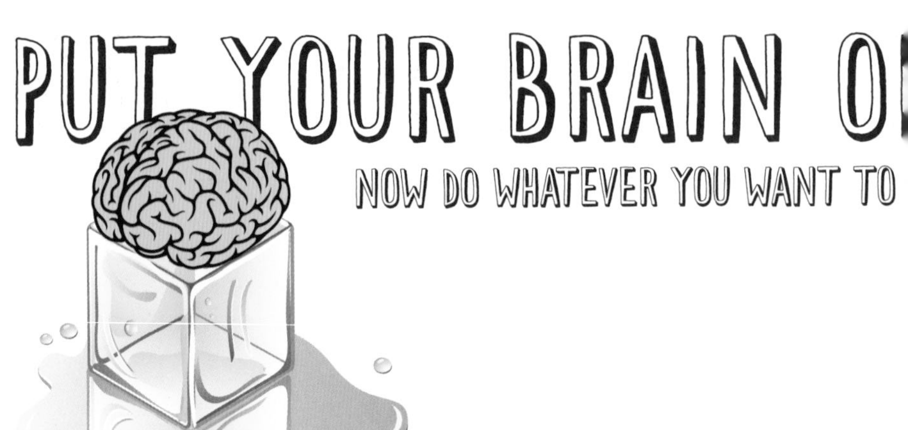
PUT YOUR BRAIN O
NOW DO WHATEVER YOU WANT TO

CE AND CHILL, BRO.

SE PAGES. WRITE ON 'EM. DRAW SOMETHING. DESTROY!

HOW MUCH $
WOULD A DUDE
HAVE TO GIVE YOU
IF HE DARED YOU
TO BRUSH
YOUR
WITH . . .

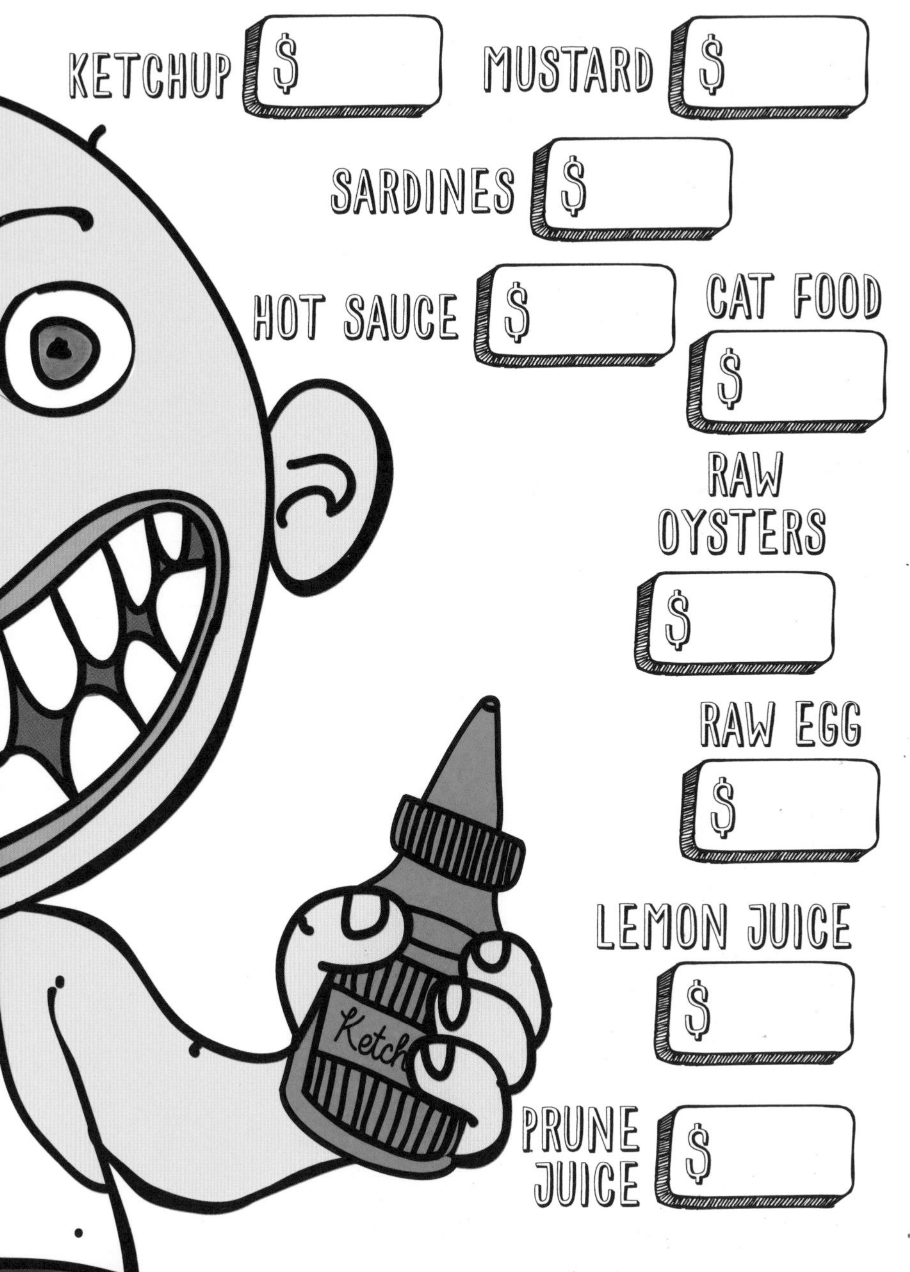
KETCHUP $
MUSTARD $
SARDINES $
HOT SAUCE $
CAT FOOD $
RAW OYSTERS $
RAW EGG $
LEMON JUICE $
PRUNE JUICE $
Ketch

YOU ARE IN CHARGE OF COMING UP WITH THE NEXT HAIRCUT AND FACIAL HAIRSTYLE FOR DUDES EVERYWHERE.

DRAW
IT

TRICK OUT THIS DASH WITH INS
DRAW THEM ON THE DASH
SCRATCH YOUR IDEAS DOWN HERE
Saltwater aquarium full of electric eels.

ELY AWESOME

AUTOMOTIVE FEATURES

WHAT WOULD BE AWESOME TO TOSS INTO THIS GIANT WEB?

BROCCOLI.
THOSE SHOES MY MOM WEARS.

MAKE UP A NEW MONTH!

1. NAME IT. 2. NUMBER, LETTER, OR MAKE UP SYMBOLS FOR EVERY DAY OF THE MONTH.

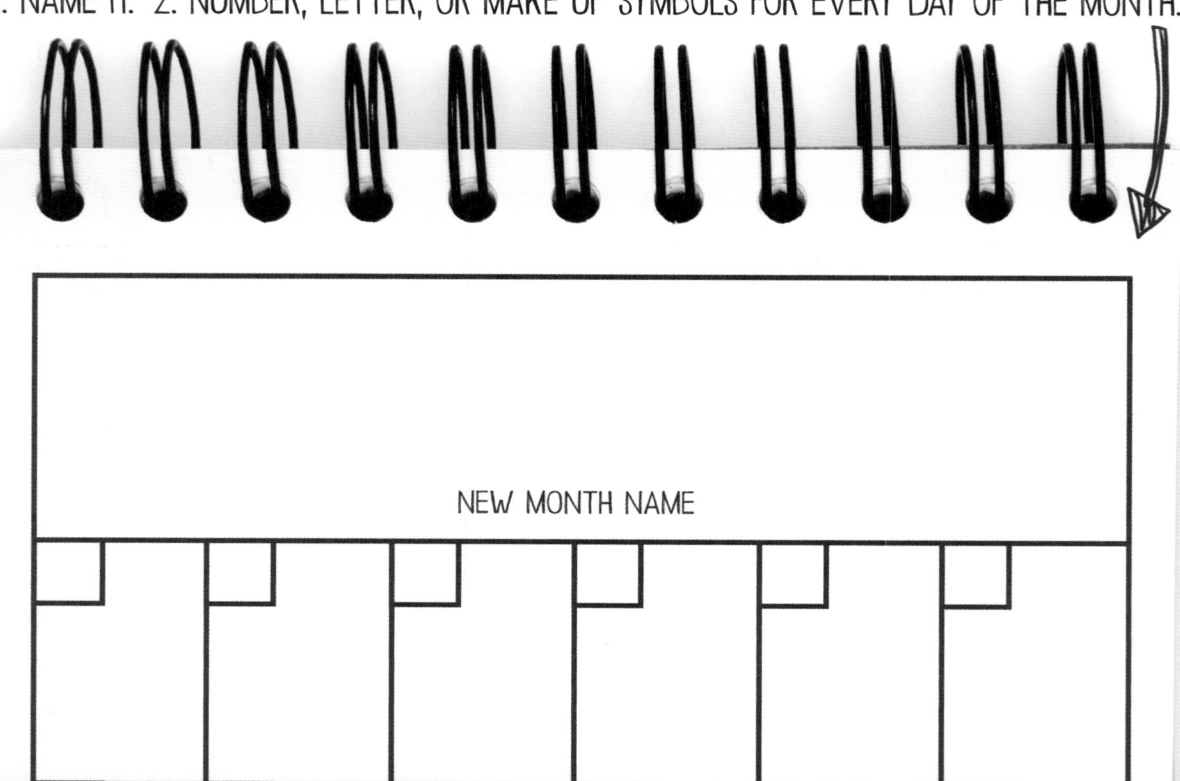

NOW ADD A BUNCH OF AWESOME HOLIDAYS TO YOUR NEW MONTH!

IF YOU WERE IN CHARGE WHO OR WHAT WOULD BE A HILARIOUS MASCOT FOR YOUR SCHOOL?

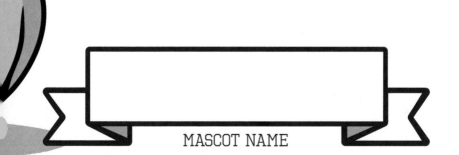

MASCOT NAME

ALL KINDS OF WRONG AWAIT YOU. TURN THE PAGE AND MANUALLY LOG IN THE STUFF THAT CLOGS UP YOUR BRAIN.

YOU'LL FREE UP SPACE FOR MORE BRILLIANTLY CRAZY IDEAS.

WRITE! DRAW! DESTROY!

Ahh, I'm a breath of death air!

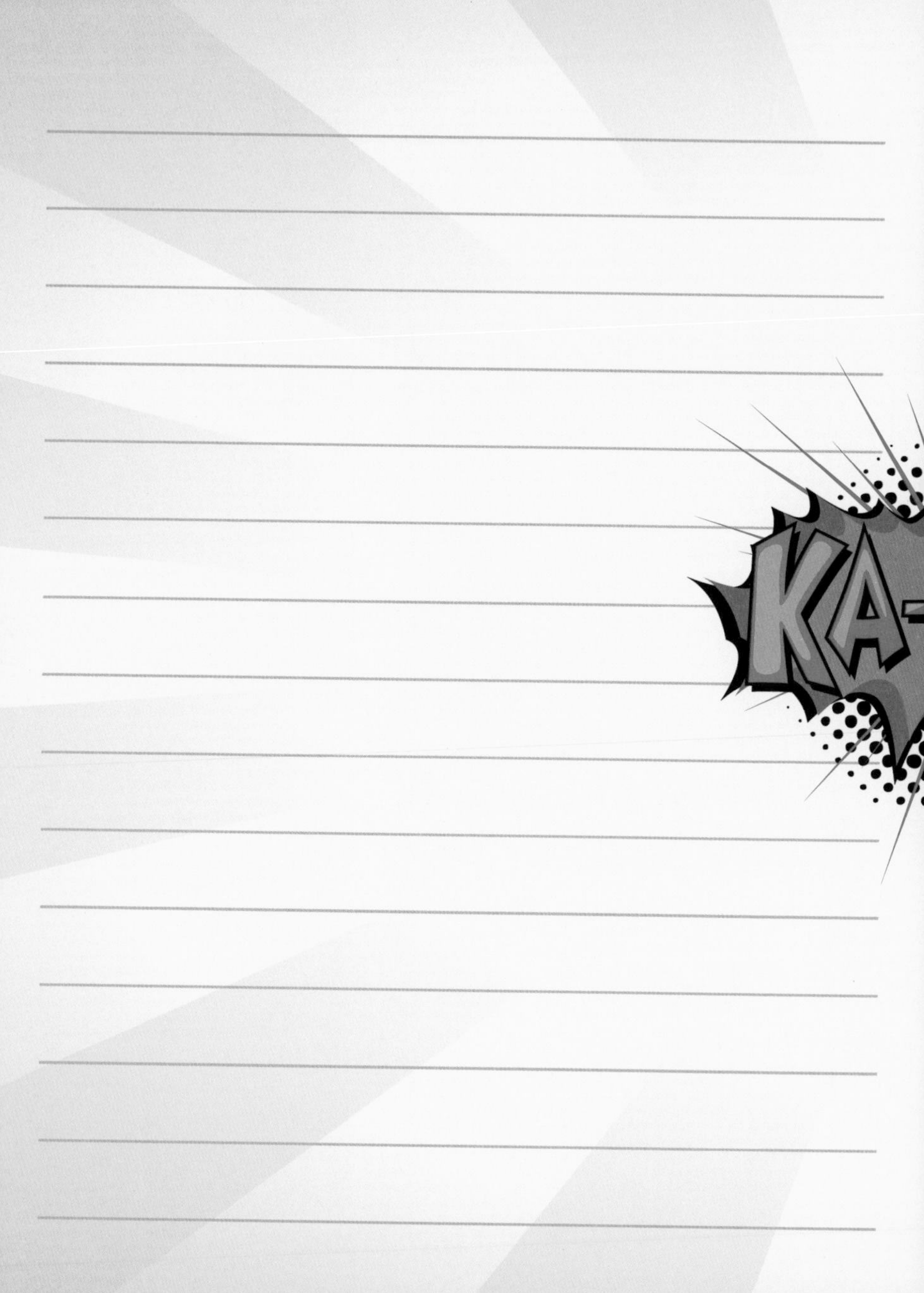
KA-

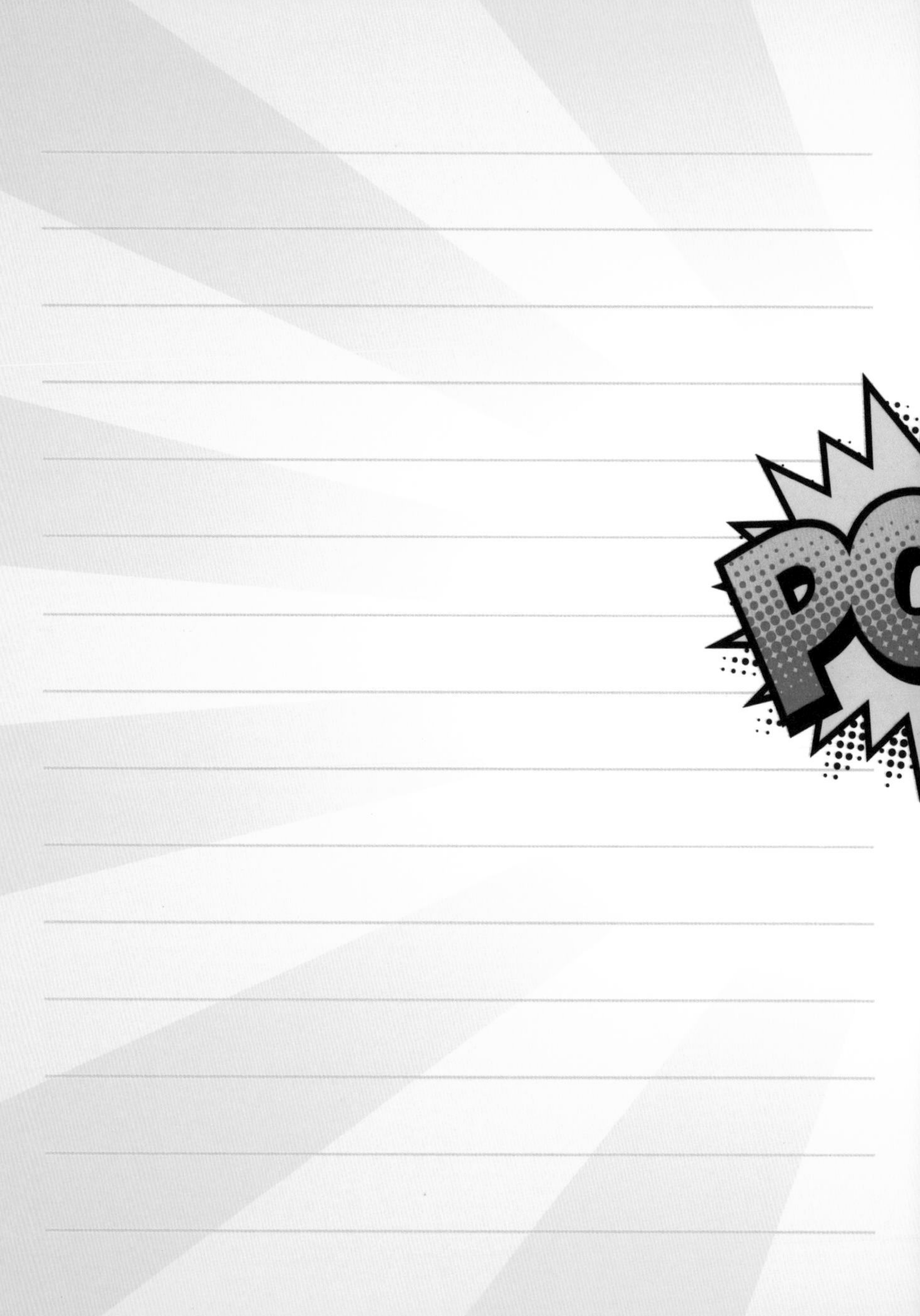

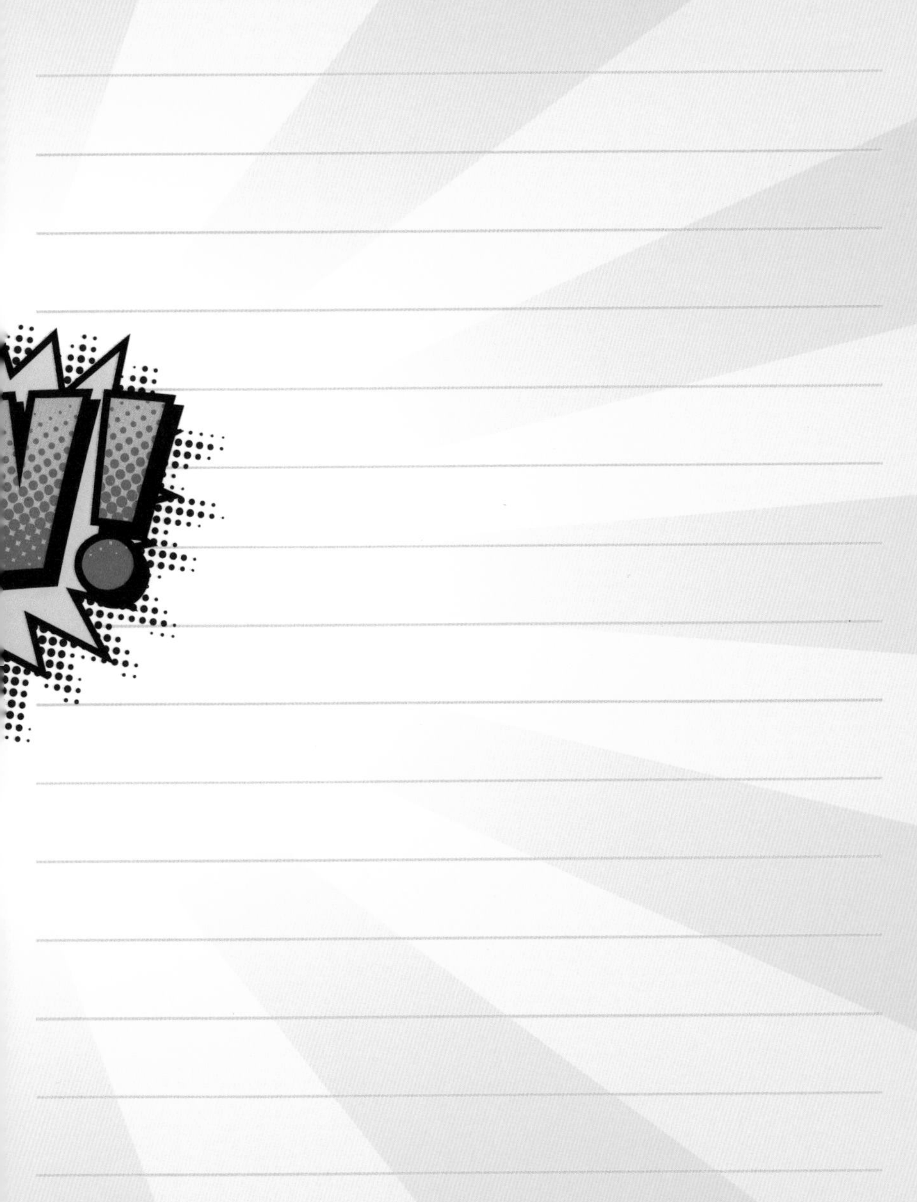

Creepfrog's
sick, bro!

This is bone-grinding, dude!

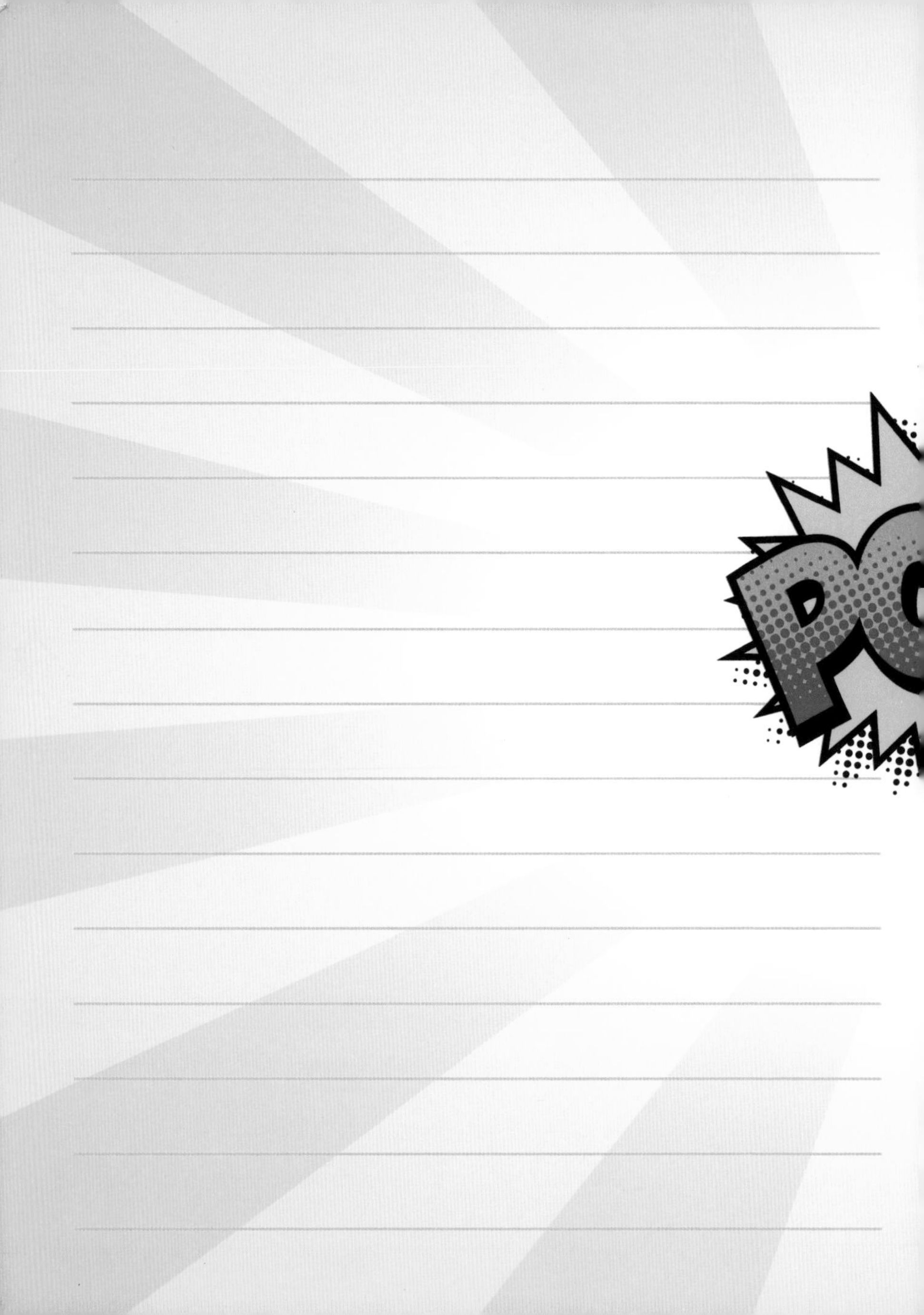

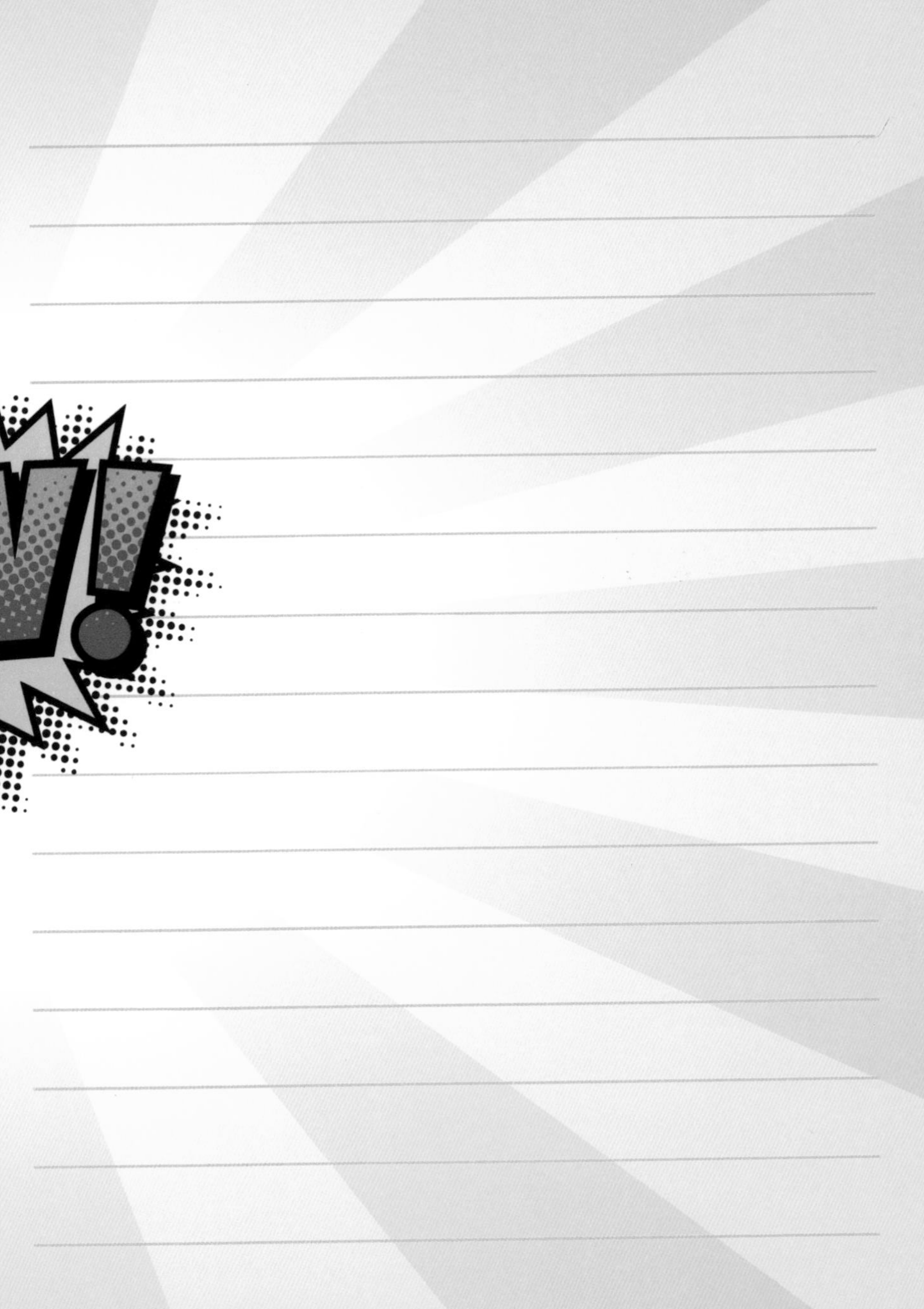

Yeah! I never felt so alive!

I like

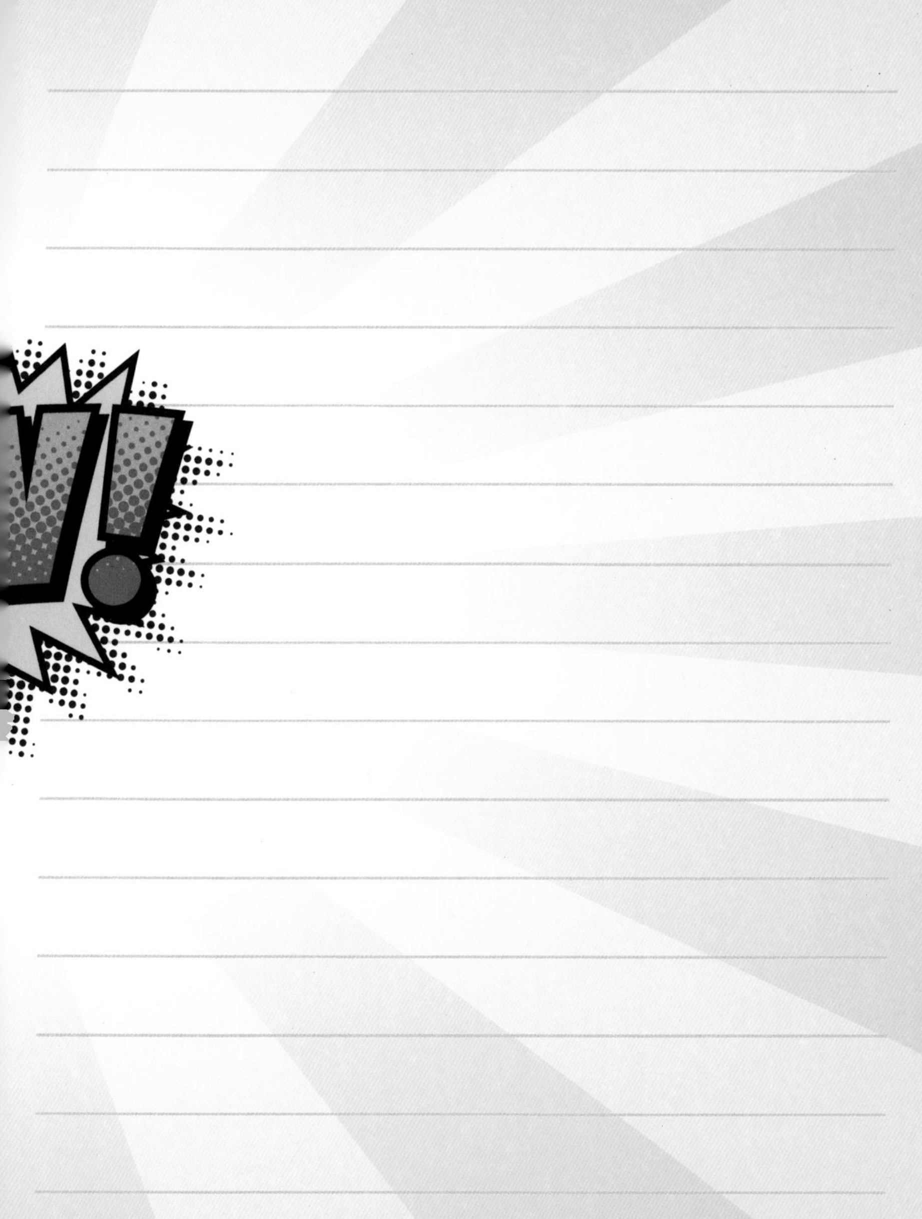

I Lik.

GAME
OVER!

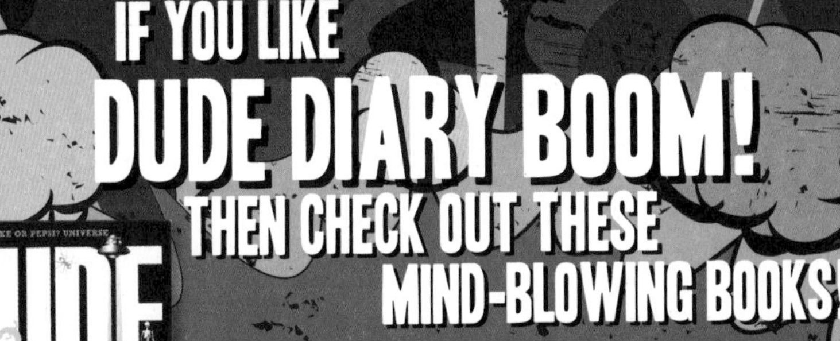

GO TO THEDUDEBOOK.COM FOR MORE CRAZY BRO STUFF!

2023 HEB-D04
EPIC W